The
Irish
Secret Agent

By
Nicholas O'Hare

Harkaway
Ireland

ISBN 0-9551563-0-0

Other books by Nicholas O'Hare

Fiction:

A Spy in Dublin
The Boyle Inheritance
The Ballylally Races
Unlawful Secrets

Equestrian:

King of Diamonds
The Modern Irish Draught
The Irish Sport Horse
The Modern Connemara

Printed and bound by Antony Rowe Ltd, Eastbourne

Chapter One

Muldowney was a secret agent. He was also a civil servant. In the structured world of Irish bureaucracy the two roles were not necessarily in conflict, but Muldowney chafed at the fact that his role as a covert defender of the institutions of the state was demeaned by humdrum job description. The civil service was for clerks and custodians of filing cabinets, for mediocre people who lived out their working lives in depressing cupboard spaces along dingy corridors. To link his profession with such pedestrian nine to fivers was an affront to Muldowney's evaluation of his chosen career.

Muldowney had a highly personalized view of his status. Filling out forms and answering telephone calls from plaintive citizens in search of unascertained and unasserted rights were no longer amongst his daily chores. Being a secret agent was very definitely something special. But it had shortcomings. It was all too secret for one thing. The glamour that should have surrounded him was absent because no one knew that he was glamorous. He didn't even have a gun, although in compensation he had a special card which identified him as a special officer of Queally's Section.

Special Officer. That was how the Section described its secret agents. His card, however, although designed to identify him, gave nothing away. There was no space for his photograph because to have it stuck on passport style would be to destroy the very ingredient of secrecy which his job demanded. All his card carried, in fact, was his name, written in ink, the word Official, and the state's silent but evocative harp.

Muldowney would have liked to have had his picture on his ID card. It would, he thought, have added considerably to his prestige. He would also have liked to be able to show it to people. The opportunities were rare. Only once in several months had he managed to thrust it into a suspect's face to demonstrate that he personified the power of the state. The suspect had turned out to be not a suspect at all, but the luckless new tenant of a flat where a notorious quarry had once resided.

At least Muldowney liked to think that the man he had gone in search of was notorious. The fact that the visit was prompted by an anonymous telephone call suggesting at the very least that the flat was a venue for clandestine meetings of smugglers, timid socialist subversives, or pornographers, was of little consolation when Muldowney found that the bird had flown.

Smugglers of condoms and banned books and magazines, were keynote targets in the Section. They could only be restrained by constant vigilance. Muldowney had been warned about this need for vigilance on the very first day in his new job, a raw recruit from Social Welfare. Queally, the diligent mastermind of the Section, and stern guardian of its secrets, had spent at least twenty minutes of his welcoming interview warning him to be vigilant. Suspects were everywhere, in business, academia, even perhaps amongst the higher echelons of the civil service itself, and without question amongst politicians.

The message was to be repeated regularly over the early months of Muldowney's apprenticeship. The fact that very little hard evidence of wrongdoing ever actually came to light did not in any way diminish the exhortations. The public deplored profiting through insider knowledge, receiving tip offs about ministerial decisions, or backscratching for state grants and often demanded action. Queally's Section officially was not interested. These activities, although deplorable were not crimes warranting the interest of secret agents or indeed anyone else. They were an Irish way of life.

Queally, however, believed in the stockpiling of all misdemeanours. He professed that even modest achievement by a citizen necessitated investigation of methods and motivation. Queally operated within strict moral and pecuniary parameters which he believed should not only govern those in his own Section but also the public at large. He was a specialist, well fashioned in the mode of the Grim Grey Men who had ruled the state for so many years.

It was this perverse outlook that had in fact provided Queally with the entire foundation for his operations. Despite appearances, despite the bald uncontroversial nature of any report into any action of a suspect, the Section never accepted that innocence was abroad. This was the core of Queally's formidable reputation. The master spy was so masterful that the fact that his spying brought so little result was in itself conclusive evidence that there was still a result out there to be obtained.

Queally's section was a special service, outside the mainstream of official secret services which the state utilized for its protection. No one knew how the Section had been created, or indeed how Queally had become its head. It was, of course, a secret. Somewhere in the distant past Queally had obviously been given command. Once he too must have had his superiors, but no one knew who they were. Queally had always been there, heading a secret institution of the state, apparently responsible to no one. Occasionally on his own initiative he briefed senior figures in the government, not as an employee, but as a mandarin who apparently wielded as much power as they very heads of government that he purported to serve.

From the outset, Muldowney had been left in no doubt as to where he stood and how he was to conduct himself. Being a secret agent meant that everything evolved in secret. The crimes were secret, the criminals were secret, and the sleuths and their investigations were secret also. Secrecy in fact prevailed throughout the whole existence of the Section and its three man team. Women were not recruited. They were untrustworthy. There was no correspondence. There were no staff records. There was no inter-office transfer of collected data. The files were maintained by Queally himself. Only Queally was in a position to co-ordinate and evaluate the information painstakingly collected by his subordinates.

Muldowney had spent several years in Social Welfare and worked his way through the ranks of disinterested colleagues to become an inspector in charge of rooting out false benefit claimants. It wasn't by any means an onerous task. Although scrupulously following the regulations, Muldowney often secretly felt that spurious or not, the claimants deserved to get the money. However, he never allowed personal sentiment to cloud his judgment. He knew that the civil service did not countenance such misheld discretion. His diligence in the course of time brought him the curious reward of a transfer to Queally's office.

This method of recruitment was one of Queally's many peculiarities of operation. He never looked for staff from the ranks of the police or the trained investigation personnel of the Revenue or the Customs, but sought out apparently under qualified candidates from the more mundane sectors of the administration. Their primary qualities seemed to be that they were diligent, effacing, and without too much predisposition to question either their superiors or the efficiency of the procedures in which they were engaged.

Although subsumed in the culture of the civil service, Muldowney had not entirely buried the stirrings of ambition, and there was a part of him that yearned for more intelligent and fulfilling duties. His early years of systematic snooping into people's lives and their miserable preoccupations with excess children, abusive spouses, and inability ever to obtain employment had sharpened Muldowney's investigative talents. He had imbibed the methodology of routine and unflinching recording of meaningless data. He had mastered the art of writing uninspiring reports in the prescribed manner, providing the essential facts but omitting any colour and sympathy which might give a human insight into human conditions.

Queally had spent longer than usual on selecting Muldowney, regarding his potential new recruit with the minimal measure of enthusiasm which he allowed himself on such occasions. It was important that he got hold of steady people. They had to have some degree of intelligence. They had to have a flair for detection and elicitation of information and casual and apparently vacuous conversation. They had to be prepared to endure long hours without complaint or any overtime pay, but above all they had to have a limited amount of ambition.

Queally had lost operatives in the past to other intelligence units, purely because his men had got too enthused with their own abilities. Now he made sure that his office was not a recruiting ground for other operations. Queally wanted his people to spend their most useful working time with him. Then when finally too disinterested and disillusioned to carry out any further effective probing, they could be returned to the muzzling shroud of mainstream civil administration.

Muldowney had been the best part of a year with the Section before Queally gave him his first major assignment. It wasn't that Queally had no faith in his new recruit. Far from it. The master spy had regaled several idle moments by contemplating the fact that once again he had reached into the morass of the state administrative machine and plucked out the best possible contender. Muldowney's lack of major assignment, however was due to the fact that there was no major assignment to assign.

That situation changed on a Tuesday morning in February. Muldowney as usual joined his colleagues in the Section

7

promptly at nine. Queally was already installed. He was always in situ, no matter how early anyone might arrive. Indeed it was believed that he lived there permanently. There was a room with a communicating door from Queally's office that was never opened in anyone's presence. Here the spymaster was reputed to retire on nights when pressure of work had kept him too late to go to his home. No one knew where home was. No one had ever been inside the closed room. Whether Queally ever left the office at night was immaterial to the fact that he was always there each morning and was still in place when they left.

The Section was located at the top of the historic General Post Office building which was still shrouded in revolutionary legend. Their floor housed part of the state wireless service but most of the rest of the building was utilized by legions of post office clerks and drably uniformed postal officials. Sometimes at night Muldowney would pass the columned granite fronted building and peer up at Queally's office. The light was always on, but the blinds were always drawn. Queally was not available for casual glimpsing by any passerby on the far side of the street, or indeed by the probing of binoculars. In Muldowney's highly coloured and embellished profile of his job, there was always the threat of the heavy jolt of a rifle bullet. To Muldowney this was not too fanciful a mid nineteen fifties echo of the angry fusillades which had peppered the building when occupied by the doomed and soulful heroes of the early part of the century.

On this morning, which at outset had seemed no different from any other, Muldowney was standing at the main office window looking down at the busy street below. Nelson's Pillar loomed at him to the left dividing the street into two lanes of only mildly chaotic traffic, horse drawn drays mingling with green buses and a varied assortment of motorcars and vans. He looked up at the statue of England's one eyed admiral on his plinth in the centre of De Valera's Ireland and tried to recollect how many steps led up to the parapet,. Was it 165 or 166. He couldn't remember.

He had climbed them once, on the day that he had joined Queally's Section. At lunchtime, in the turbulence of his appointment and the vista of excitement and achievement which he then envisaged, he had paid sixpence to the caretaker and gone up the winding dank stone steps to the top in a bid to clear his head. He could remember looking towards the statue of the Liberator, O'Connell and the wide bridge cross the Liffey which bore his name and then walking round the balcony to stare back down the wide street to the Parnell monument and the Rotunda behind it.

He had once looked at the inscription on Parnell's memorial. Something about no man halting the march of a nation, he reflected.

That first day in the job, at Nelson's feet high above the city, he genuinely believed that no man would stop the march of Muldowney in the service of the state. Had he been more intuitively reflective, he might perhaps have contemplated the fact that while in death Parnell had been given a public place on the city street, he had been mocked and hounded to that death by the very people that he had striven to serve.

But today Muldowney had only a fleeting interest in Parnell and his troubles. There would no doubt be troubles enough in the office workload once the Director got stuck into the business of the day. Below him the city's workers scurried to their jobs, paper sellers were hawking the morning editions, the inevitable winter rain drizzled down on Dublin as it did on almost every other morning.

Muldowney's casual study of the city's main thoroughfare was interrupted by a curt command from Queally's doorway.

He glimpsed the rounded, late middle aged, bespectacled figure of the spymaster for a second, went rapidly to his desk and picked up his current files. His colleague, Cronin, was doing the same thing. They had both been summoned in sharp commanding tones, underlined with more than the Director's usual acerbity.

They stood together in front of Queally's desk. There were chairs on one side of the room, but there was no invitation to use them. Queally was not a believer in having people sit. They thought bestr on their feet, he maintained, and got through meetings in half the time. Cronin was fidgeting with his file, but Muldowney kept his under his arm. He sensed that their meeting had nothing to do with ongoing enquiries.

"Close that thing up," Queally growled at Cronin, a big burly man, very much like a beat policeman, but who had in fact come to the Section by way of the census office of the Department of Agriculture.

Cronin dropped some sheets of paper in a briefly agitated response to the Director's command, but quickly whipped them up from the floor and like Muldowney tucked the files under his arm.

"We've an important mission," Queally told them. "It is difficult, dangerous, and must be conducted with the utmost secrecy."

Difficulties and secrets were well used words in the Director's vocabulary. But it was the first time that Queally had ever spoken to Muldowney of danger. Muldowney's senses quickened. Here at last was a whiff of the real stuff of a secret agent's lifestyle. Finally he was going to get a taste of what such a career was all about.

Queally stared him directly in the face. It was not usually his

10

way to meet a man's eye, but this was an occasion when the full force of authority had to be impressed upon his subordinate.

"You're going undercover, Muldowney," he said.

He opened a drawer and brought out a sheet of paper, placing it carefully on the desk in front of him.

"You'll be in deep cover for quite a long time.

Queally tapped the sheet of paper with a forefinger. Muldowney screwed up is eyes but he couldn't read the text. However, the red stamp on the top was more than legible. He had expected to read the word SECRET. Most of Queally's documents were branded that way. He had the rubber stamp and pad on the desk in front of him at all times. This time, whoever, there was a difference. The caution consisted of two words – TOP SECRET.

"This mission is highly sensitive," Queally went on. "No one outside this room is to know of its existence. It is not to be discussed with anyone."

He fixed Muldowney with his full frontal stare once again.

"When you leave the office to take up this duty you will not return until the mission is completed. Neither will you go back to your accommodation or make any contact with your friends or family. You are to take up a totally new identity. Every other contact or liaison that you have is to be terminated immediately."

Liaison and terminate were two more of Queally's favourite and often repeated words. Muldowney suspected that he gained some form of sensual gratification from the use of the word liaison, endowing it perhaps with an implication of illicit contact with women. He wondered if his use of the word terminate had a more sinister aspect. Had Queally ever terminated anyone? Muldowney switched his attention back to the Director once more.

"You will make contact with me through Cronin," Queally was saying. He will be your controller and your only link with the Section."

This procedure was again a tried and trusted Queally method of operation. He always kept himself at one remove from an operative in the field. That way he ensured that he was protected as much as possible from any failure or difficulty with the enquiry. Queally made sure that he ran his operations with as little administrative liability or personal career damage as possible.

"What is the mission, sir," Muldowney asked.

Queally frowned. Muldowney was more than half prepared to hear that it was yet another secret, but Queally allowed himself to reveal that the agent would get full instructions once he had settled into his new identity.

"You are to spend the next twenty four hours getting yourself set up with an undercover base," Queally ordered. "Cronin will drive you to Cork and you will come back to Dublin on the train just as if you were arriving in the city for the first time. You will draw a month's pay and sufficient for expenses in advance, but you cannot presume to live at a higher standard than your normal salary allows."

Even in the face of this secret and possibly dangerous duty, the usual financial controls would apply. Queally's Section after all was a division of the administration and its personnel had to conduct themselves like all other civil servants. Being a designated secret agent did not imply that there could be any profligate distribution of government funds.

Queally was talking to Cronin now. The big man moved uneasily from one foot to the other, but it soon became apparent that whatever tribulations Muldowney might have to undergo in the pursuit of whatever investigation was to be launched, Cronin's role would be infinitely less arduous. It would also apparently be considerably safer. Cronin was to remain at his desk, apply himself to his usual work, but take fixed time calls every morning which Muldowney would make from a public call box.

Queally finally nodded dismissal, but Muldowney decided to ask one more question.

"Is this a dangerous mission, sir."

Queally frowned.

"All undercover missions are dangerous," he said. "You must not allow yourself to be exposed."

Muldowney forebore to remark that since he didn't know what the mission was about, nor whom he was going undercover to locate, concealment might be a problem. The quarry might locate the hunter first. It would be difficult to take more than the elementary precaution of changing his name and address. He asked what he felt was the really pertinent question of the briefing.

"What I mean, sir," he said hesitantly. "Is do I draw a weapon as well as my expense allowance."

Cronin went rigid as a board. He had never even heard of weapons being issued in the Section, but Queally appeared to

13

consider the matter carefully.

"Have you had any weapons training," he asked eventually, blinking through his glasses at his eager subordinate.

Muldowney's heart sank, visions of wearing a shoulder holster and a tell tale underarm bulge rapidly evaporating.

"No, sir," he replied. "I'm afraid not. We didn't use guns in Social Welfare."

Queally picked up his sheet of top secret paper and swished it back into his drawer.

"You've answered your own question then," he said. Untrained men can't have weapons."

Queally folded his arms and stared down at his empty desk. The briefing was definitely over. Cronin was the first to move for the door, glad to have escaped with so little responsibility thrust upon his shoulders.

Muldowney walked slowly after him, also relieved that the interview was over, but an unruly thought probed his brain. Just what action could an unarmed secret agent take if he ran into the unspecified secret dangers which the spymaster had warned lurked around this and indeed all undercover operations.

Chapter Two

Muldowney arrived back in Dublin on the evening train from Cork. The likelihood was that he was walking through Kingsbridge station before Cronin had got the aging Section car as far back to the city as Kildare or Newbridge, but he no longer had any interest in his fellow agent's whereabouts. The priority now was to find a place to stay. A flat was the most suitable option but that would take time. A bed and breakfast or a very cheap hotel would get him over the first night.

He stood on the bridge looking into the dark waters of the Liffey and savoured the wonderful smell of cooked barley coming from the giant brewery. Two blue Guinness barges were moored to bollards waiting to be loaded with barrels of black beer which would be brought down river to the tiny ships named after the Guinness ladies which waited for the English tide on the far side of O'Connell bridge.

He debated momentarily as to which side of the river he would walk. The left would set him for the northside, the right would take him to the more affluent and socially acceptable south side. Ever conscious of the need for prudence, he walked across the bridge to the left, passed the military barracks with its great glowering Crimea cannon squatting on a square of grass, turned into cobbled Smithfield, once a large market and still a location for harness, hay and horse feeds, and headed towards Capel street, home of cheap clothes shops and pawnbrokers.

He walked on, away from the quays, and started to reach mainly residential streets. The houses were small but neat, dating from a more pretentious Victorian era which demonstrated the solid values with a lot of red brick, even for the working classes. There were no signs offering room or board, and it was a part of the city which had no hotels either. Realising that he might walk on for miles and not find a place to stay, he turned into a pub to make enquiries.

There was, it transpired, a boarding house a couple of streets away, clean and inexpensive. The information came from a girl at the bar. She was a bit flashy for Muldowney's taste, cheaply dressed with long red hair, pendant earrings and heavy make-up. She had had a few drinks, Muldowney decided, and the two male companions who flanked her on each side had knocked back even more, but they were pleasant enough. Muldowney decided to take the girl at her word.

Without directions he would never have found the house. It was no different from its neighbours, dingy, with coloured glass panes in the front door panels and the inevitable net curtains of the period obscuring the windows. The woman, Mrs Conroy, showed him to an upstairs room. He was still in time for that evening's supper if he hurried. He paid for two nights and said that he might stay for a few days longer and would let her know.

Muldowney washed and changed his jacket for a sweater and then went towards the stairs. The house seemed to have been extended further back than normal and there were quite a lot of bedrooms. The owners had developed a fairly prosperous business, he decided. There was no one in the dining room yet, so he went further along the hall and walked into what was evidently the communal sitting room for all the guests. Several girls were sitting around the room. There was a record player in one corner and some magazines on a central table. A wireless was playing some light orchestral music.

As he walked in all eyes shifted to him expectantly. Muldowney liked women. He preferred their company to that of men. He liked them to be feminine, lively, stylish. The smart high heeled girls who paraded down Grafton street at lunchtime each day epitomized the young Dublin woman of his aspirations. The Grafton street girls were flaunters, he decided, in their way the vanguard of the changes which were being rung in De Valera's chaste and pleasant land. Skirts were getting slightly shorter, blouses were coming off the shoulder, and there was a great deal of thrusting robust young womanhood in display in the summer months.

He was disappointed in the boarding house girls. There were six or seven of them, all fairly plain girls, probably from the country, he decided, all dressed in fairly plain clothes as well. They looked as if they had all been to the same shop. Similar skirts and cardigans were surmounted by scrubbed faces and identical hairstyles. The faces did vary from one to the other, Muldowney admitted, but they all had an extraordinary uniform look nonetheless.

Muldowney sat down awkwardly, picking up a magazine before he did so. He was very much aware of their scrutiny. Under cover of turning the pages, he quickly studied each of the occupants. They were all fairly young, he decided, certainly not much more than seventeen or eighteen. He wondered if they were students on a course, such was the standardization of their dress and looks. Then he thought perhaps that they were all daughters or relations of the house, rather than guests, and that their outfits were due to a central purchasing policy.

One of the girls caught him looking at her over the top of the magazine and smiled. It was a smile which was pleasant enough, and seemed friendly, but somehow lacked warmth. The others had apparently lost interest and were either reading or deep in thought.

Mrs Conroy, the lady of the house, came in at that point and summoned him into the dining room for his meal. The girls made no move to join him and he assumed that they either ate at a separate sitting or went down to the kitchen for their meals, away from the paying residents.

"Do you like the girls," Mrs Conroy asked as she set down a plate of ham and salad in front of him, and reached for the teapot. He was a bit surprised at the question.

"Yes," he said. "Very pleasant."

The woman looked at him sharply, a sudden intense scrutiny, finished pouring out his tea and went towards the door.

"If there is anything you need, let me know," she said and was gone.

For a moment Muldowney felt that there was some significance to her words but immediately forgot the feeling. Another man came into the room and sat down at the far side of the table. It was set for six which was apparently the full complement of guests, although it could comfortably seat up to a dozen or more. Perhaps the girls did have their meals here, either earlier or later, Muldowney thought. Maybe their mother didn't like them to mingle too closely with the boarders.

The newcomer was disposed to talk, not that he had much to communicate. Muldowney responded automatically, glad of the company but not really interested enough to start up a conversation. Then surprisingly his companion made the same enquiry as the landlady.

"What do you think of the girls," he asked.

Muldowney frowned in momentary perplexity and made some vacuous response. The other laughed.

"They're not exactly the best looking girls in town," he said, "But the set up is good enough and not too expensive."

Muldowney agreed. The bed and breakfast rate was reasonable

and the house seemed clean and comfortable.

"I suppose there are worse places," he commented.

The other agreed strongly.

"There are indeed," he said. "Some of these joints are right kips."

There was a ring at the front door, and someone came up the corridor from the back of then house. It wasn't the landlady, possibly her husband. There was a muttered conversation, and the newcomer was admitted. He wasn't brought into the dining room, however, but evidently went straight to the sitting room. After a few moments there was some movement up the stairs.

"Business is booming," Muldowney's companion remarked. He pushed back his chair. "I'm for the pub. Do you fancy a drink."

Muldowney shook his head. He was tired after the double journey to Cork and back, and his walk through the city. Besides, he needed more time to think out his plan of campaign for the next morning. Hopefully his check call to Cronin would elicit some meaningful instructions and start him off on his mission.

The woman was in the hall when he left the dining room.

"You're not going out then," she asked.

Muldowney shook his head.

"I'm for bed," he said. "I've a heavy day tomorrow."

One of the girls came to the door of the sitting room and stood there, evidently waiting for her mother to take her attention away from the visitor. Muldowney said goodnight including each of them in his salutation. The girl met his eye and held him in her gaze until he turned away, suddenly embarrassed. The landlady apparently noticed nothing. Just as he started up the stairs a key turned in the front door and the girl from the pub came in.

Muldowney was surprised. He hadn't realized that she lived there. She was a different stamp to the rest of the girls in the house, certainly a lot more worldly, perhaps even a bit on the tarty side, Muldowney thought to himself. She compensated a great deal for the lack of style and personality of the girls in the sitting room. It was perhaps the difference between a girl born and bred in Dublin city and her country cousin.

She greeted him in a friendly manner, and jerked her head towards the landlady.

"I sent him up earlier on," she said in explanation. She turned towards Muldowney again. "You found your way alright."

Muldowney said that he had no problem and she rattled on again.

"Is there anything you need. Did you meet the girls."

At this Muldowney surmised that she too was a member of the family although she was a totally different model to the clones in the sitting room.

"The chap is going to bed," the landlady said sharply. "He's tired after coming to the city."

The red haired girl closed her eyes for a moment in a half expressed gesture of irritation and then pulled a packet of cigarettes from her pocket.   She offered one to Muldowney

20

who declined and put a foot on the next step up.

"That's it then," the girl said to the woman. "I'm going back out after I get something to eat."

They both went down the corridor towards the kitchen and Muldowney went upstairs to his room.

He was asleep when the house was raided. The noise of the front door being kicked in first brought him around. Then he heard shouts and the sound of feet pounding up the stairs. There were cries and squeals from some of the other rooms. Suddenly without any warning his own bedroom door was flung open and three blue uniformed men rushed in.

They stopped in their tracks for a second or so, evidently slightly confused, then pulled Muldowney out of bed. His protests were ignored. He was handed his jacket, trousers and shoes, and pushed outside into the corridor. In the landing light he could see that they were all policemen. The corridor was crowded with the other occupants of the rooms, men and women, half dressed. People occasionally emerged from other bedrooms, apparently having been given time to put on some sort of clothing.

His captors urged him towards the stairs and barefoot, he followed other residents down to the hall. There the landlady and a thin balding man who was evidently her husband were each standing between two officers.

Muldowney started to protest again and got a thump on his back. He half turned and looked up the stairs. As far as he could see all the plain girls were amongst the prisoners. They looked different now, tousled hair and hastily thrown on clothing had dissipated the uniformity that was so much in evidence when they sat together in the sitting room earlier on. His neighbour at supper was nearest to him. There was no sign of the red haired girl who had directed him to the house.

"What is this all about," he asked both his supper companion and any of the policemen who might care to listen.

"We're arrested," the other said. "Say nothing until you get a solicitor."

Muldowney decided to exert his authority. After all he was as much an upholder of law and order as any of the uniformed police officers.

"I demand an explanation," he stormed. It was an uncharacteristic outburst. He was ordinarily a quiet unassuming man. "Who is in charge."

A sergeant with a clipboard came up the passageway from the rear of the house.

"Name and address," he demanded.

Muldowney gave his name and suddenly remembering his cover, said that he had no address other than the boarding house.

"No fixed abode," the sergeant said aloud as he wrote the words down.

Muldowney protested again, the civil servant's ingrained respect for detail overcoming the offensiveness of his situation.

"I have residence here," he said. "I've paid for board and lodging for two nights. This is the first of them. I've just arrived in Dublin."

"You'll have a different address shortly," the sergeant

commented.

"Are we being arrested," Muldowney asked perplexedly. "I don't understand."

The sergeant motioned his officers to bring Muldowney and the landlady and her husband out through the front door. Muldowney could see a row of police cars and two large blue vans with insignia on them as well.

"You'll be charged at the station," the sergeant said. "You're under arrest for patronizing a brothel."

Muldowney was dumfounded. A brothel. He had never conceived that such an institution might be found in the overtly moral Dublin of De Valera and Archbishop John Charles McQuaid, much less that he would be found in it, and arrested for being there. He looked accusingly at his landlady, but she ignored him. They were taken outside and thrust into the first of the vans. Some of the girls and other men were brought in as well and when the seats were full, the van started off, preceded by a police car with its bell clanging.

In the police station it was clear that the arrested permanent occupants of what the law still quaintly described as a disorderly house were as surprised and disgruntled as Muldowney and the other paying guests. The male patrons, who had obviously paid for an extra tariff than that ordered by the secret agent, were openly apprehensive. They were ordinary nondescript beings. The plain girls, their surprise overcome, were noisily indignant. The madam and her husband remained outwardly calm. All of them were brought into a day room with benches down both sides.

Muldowney too quiet stock of his companions. Only one of them stood out from the rest. He was an army officer in uniform. The secret agent was not too familiar with military

23

stars and bars. Army personnel of whatever rank had seldom found their way to the Department of Social Welfare, and although they might be thought to be more likely visitors to Queally's Section, he had never encountered them there either.

In fact the only men in uniform that Muldowney had ever seen near Queally's office were the postal officials who inhabited most of the building where the Section had its hideway. Muldowney judged that because of his age this man had to be at least a commandant and possibly even a lieutenant colonel. Of them all he seemed the most distressed. He kept wiping his forehead with a pale green handkerchief, and compulsively pulling open his jacket and doing it up again.

The sergeant with the clipboard accompanied by another policeman came into the room. Muldowney decided that he had to take some action to disclose his identity and put and end to the situation. He took off his shoe and removed the insole to bring out his ID card. At the outset of his undercover role he had thought it best to conceal his credentials where secret agents conceal things best. The card had become discoloured by the heat and sweating of his feet but the harp and the bold type of the word OFFICIAL were suddenly very comforting.

The sergeant began to marshal the plain girls and their employers together prior to leaving the room. It was obviously intended that the clients and the staff of the establishment were to be separated for the purpose of taking statements. Muldowney put his foot back inn his shoe and stood up.

"Sit down," the sergeant barked at him raising his clipboard as if to administer a blow although Muldowney was several feet away from him. Muldowney collapsed on the bench. The army officer wiped his forehead again and pulled his buttoned up jacket apart once more.

"We won't be charging you men at this point," the sergeant addressed them. "But we'll more than likely call some of you as witnesses."

The army officer nearly fell off the bench in further distress, and one of the others started to cry. The policeman was unsympathetic.

"You should have thought of your families before you went to that place," he said. "We're going to verify your names and addresses and then we'll let you go."

In such a fashion did the arm of the law and indeed justice itself distinguish between those who plied their trade as purveyors of sexual favours and the clients who patronized and paid them.

Far from relieving any anxieties felt by the assembled miscreants, the sergeant's announcement provoked further disquiet. The last thing any of them wanted was for the police to go to their homes. It was at this point that Muldowney noticed that his supper companion was not amongst the dozen or so men in the room.

"If any one has acceptable identification," the sergeant suddenly relented, "we can take it instead of calling to your homes."

One or two of them produced some documents and Muldowney held out his card as the sergeant walked past, turning his back on his nearest neighbour to ensure that no prying eye could ascertain what it was that he was offering to the policeman. Whatever about showing his ID to the police at this time, Muldowney was certain that his duty as a secret agent must ensure that it should not be needlessly shown to casual members of the public, even if they did appear to be sharing with him the heavy handed weight of the law.

The sergeant frowned at the card and then at Muldowney.

"Have you any other documentation," he asked.

Muldowney shook his head.

"Where do you live," the policeman demanded.

Muldowney said again what he had originally said at the boarding house. He had just arrived in the city and it was his only address.

The sergeant dropped a strong hand on his shoulder, displaying the effectiveness and easy application of a grip well used to arresting wrongdoers.

"You'd better come with me," he said. "We'll have to make further enquiries about you."

This was not the kind of response Muldowney had expected to get from producing his ID. Irritated but obedient he followed the sergeant out of the room. The man who had been his supper companion at the brothel was leaning across the front desk of the station talking to the uniformed officer on the other side.

For the first time since he had gone undercover, Muldowney's burgeoning and specially cultivated secret agent's rapid response system came into play. He understood immediately that here was the real undercover man at the scene of the crime. The police had sent in a plainclothes advance man prior to the raid. The sergeant handed Muldowney's card to the detective. He looked at it briefly and handed it directly back to Muldowney.

"What were you doing there," he asked conversationally.

26

Muldowney realized that he had met a fellow specialist who was immediately able to grasp the essential facts of the situation.

Now well back into his role as one of Queally's special secret operatives, Muldowney's mental rapid response system went into overdrive. He had to discard the real truth behind his appearance at this most unfortunate choice of residence and come up with a much more compelling but nonetheless fictionalized version of events.

"I was carrying out surveillance on the army officer," he said in a brilliant flash of expediency, the future perfection of which would certainly take him far in his secretive career. The detective whistled softly.

"Were you indeed."

He took the clipboard from the sergeant.

"John Dominic O'Connor," he read out. "He's a colonel, based at the Curragh."

Muldowney congratulated himself. He hadn't been too far wrong in his earlier assessment of the rank of the military man who caught in a house of ill repute by the ordinary law had now become an official target of his secret department's surveillance.

"What do you want us to do with him," the detective asked.

Muldowney thought for a moment.

"I want to get close to him without arousing suspicion," he improvised. "The best thing to do would be to release both of us together and we can get a taxi back to the boarding house. I suppose we can get in," he remarked in sudden alarm. "My things are there."

"Good thinking," the detective said, overlooking this unprofessional concern for the mundane contents of a suitcase and indicating his approval for the ruse. "You can both put up for the rest of the night there. He was booked in as a guest as well. We won't stop you using the room for the rest of the night."

Muldowney forebore to remark that he had paid for his lodgings, brothel or no brothel, and was quite entitled at least to use the domestic facilities even if the other services of the establishment were to be denied to him.

"We'll let Mrs Conroy go so that she can open up the house as well," the detective went on ruminatively. "But we're holding the girls and her husband. They'll go direct to the district court in the morning. Unless, of course, you have any objection to Mrs Conroy being let go," the detective added hastily.

Muldowney rightly took this as recognition of an enhanced status. The detective was now treating him as a superior officer.

"Yes, let the woman out," he said, mentally adducing that at least there would be someone there to make the breakfast in the morning. He kept this assessment of the situation to himself. After all, secret agents of his calibre were not normally seduced by breakfast, even breakfast in a colourful establishment such as that run by Mrs Conroy. He accepted some further boost to his self esteem with the reflection that he had not been seduced by any of the brothel's inmates either. It was a reflection tinged with regret but at the same time he felt that to have succumbed to the charms of one of the plain girls would have been a long way short of interaction with exotic femmes fatales from the world of espionage and subversion.

28

Chapter Three

The police gave the entrepreneurial landlady a half hour start before letting Muldowney and the still distraught army officer out on the streets as well. Muldowney went through the charade of signing the station bail bond in the presence of the soldier adding more authenticity to his role as a comrade in adversity. There was no sign of a taxi and they walked back through the dimly lighted streets to the now less than welcoming shelter of Mrs Conroy's establishment.

The colonel spent most of the time lamenting his admittedly perilous situation. To be caught in such circumstances was hardly likely to improve his chances of promotion. Indeed if there was any publicity in the newspapers, he might well be cashiered. Muldowney comforted his companion with the reassurance that the episode was most unlikely to be reported. Nothing that smacked of moral deviance ever got past the sub-editors' desk in Irish newspapers. The weekly purveyors of smut published on the far side of the Irish Sea were discouraged and sometimes banned from entering Ireland's pristine shores. Without such decadent competition Irish press and Irish people would lead their lives unsullied by reprehensible reportage.

State and Church deemed it in the best interest of national integrity that the common people should never learn that there were Irishmen who beat their wives into submission, imposed themselves on their daughters, or sought the services of ladies of the night if lawful bedroom opportunity was not available.

The institutions of the state, one of which Muldowney served so selflessly, were all united in preserving the censored integrity of the island of saints and scholars. Neither Muldowney nor the Grim Grey Men who ruled the green island had as yet any foretaste of the fact that time would soon be called on this remarkable piece of Celtic mysticism. Yet soon, almost overnight, it would be realized that the scholars had driven out the saints and that St Patrick's cast out serpents had in reality been hiding under the shamrock leaves all the time. The comforting restrains of guaranteed privacy for every type of deviation which were imposed in deference to public moral susceptibilities would be struck down. The day would surely come when delinquent colonels and other miscreant apparent pillars of society would be exposed for what they were.

For the moment, however, the colonel was safe as far as exposure in the newspapers was concerned. Evidently Muldowney's reassurances gave him some comfort. The coolness of the night air also calmed him sufficiently to allow the military mind to take more realistic stock of his situation.

"What I need is a drink," the gallant scion of the defence forces decided.

Muldowney was thinking the same thing, not that he himself needed the stimulus of alcohol, but he thought that some conviviality might get him into a more subtle bonding with his companion. After all, he reasoned, to get a good working relationship up and running with the military had to be to the advantage of the Section. It was not inconceivable that this relationship could be a vital cog in the furtherance of his mission. A disturbing momentary thought reminded Muldowney that he did not yet know what his mission was.

He dismissed the twinge of self doubt and looked at his watch. It was a quarter to four, another five hours must elapse before he had to make his first fixed time call at nine o'clock to Cronin waiting at headquarters. The colonel noticed his movement and put his own interpretation on it.

"You're right," he said. "We'll get a pub open at the cattle market."

THE IRISH SECRET AGENT

Muldowney knew nothing of Dublin's curious licensing laws that allowed public houses to open at five o'clock in the morning to quench the thirst of cattle drovers but he followed obediently. For the moment, control of the operation had fallen into the hands of the military. It was a situation, Muldowney determined, which would not be allowed to continue for too long.

They were well esconced in the drovers' lair and had several whiskeys inside them when the plain clothed sleuth from the supper table the previous evening arrived as well. He bought a pint of stout at the bar, caught sight of them, came across and drew up a chair at their table.

The sight of the detective demoralized the colonel once again. He swallowed the last of his whiskey and leaning back in his chair, closed his eyes in the hope that lowered eyelids would drive his enemy away. The detective leaned across the table to Muldowney.

"I'll push this fella bit for you," he whispered. "We'll give him a taste of good cop, bad cop."

Muldowney was too surprised to object, and after a moment's reflection decided that he had no option but to go along with the proposal. He couldn't tell his new found colleague that the colonel was a fortuitous target, conjured out of the air to bolster his own unsatisfactory alibi. Anyway, all they seemed likely to elicit was a spate of further terrors about problems with his superiors and his family.

The detective tapped the table with his glass.

"I want some answers from you," he snapped.

The colonel stared at him mesmerized. The policeman pointed an accusing finger.

"We know everything," he said. "So there is no point in you telling us lies."

Muldowney marveled at the detective's interrogatory technique. "Everything" was an exceptionally comprehensive description of information possessed by a suspect who just happened to have taken his trousers off in an abode also patronised by a secret agent.

He decided to take a hand in the interview and brought out his sweat stained ID for the second time that night. He gave the colonel a practiced flash of the card, perfected by many rehearsals in front of his bathroom mirror and put it back in his pocket.

To his surprise the army officer responded in even more desperation than when barracked by the detective.

"Alright, alright," he burst out. "I'll tell you everything I know."

For the next few minutes Muldowney and the detective listened spellbound to the penitent colonel's confession. When he had finished they stared at him in amazement. The detective brought out a notebook and a stubby pencil but Muldowney put a hand on his arm.

"This case belongs to my Section," he said. "The information confirms my investigations. What has been said here must go no further. But I'll see that you get full credit in my report," he added generously.

The detective reluctantly put his writing materials away. Muldowney sought to relieve his disappointment.

"You'll be well in line for promotion," he promised. "Perhaps even a transfer to the Service."

They sat for a few moments in silence, each concerned only with his own personal reactions to the comments of his companions. Muldowney glanced quickly around the pub. It was a typical Dublin hostelry, heavy mahogany counter with brass footrail, dark wooden panels around the walls topped by a selection of aging embossed mirrors advertising brands of beers and spirits going back into the previous century. Some of the occupants looked as if they were of that vintage as well, Muldowney decided. They were the dirtiest, most disheveled bunch of muck booted red faced country folk he had ever seen in the city. They were armed with a collection of sticks that would have done credit to a tinkers' faction fight. The place had its own distinctive cattle linked odour as well.

Muldowney now had a serious problem. The outpourings of the downcast colonel had given a new dimension to his operation. Quite by chance he had stumbled on a situation and a suspect that gave credence to his mission. Later on when he made his fixed time check call he would be reporting to Queally that not only had he gone undercover successfully but that he had unearthed an extraordinary breach of national security.

They were listening to an incredible tale. The woeful colonel was part of a conspiracy to steal state owned gold which was being sent to London by the government. He wasn't the main man by any means. There were unknown important figures at the top. O'Connor had a relatively minor role. He was the officer detailed to command the military escort from the Central Bank vault to the airport. The gold would be stolen on his watch. It was an outrageous, stupendous tale. Not for a long time, Muldowney believed, had a Section agent succeeded so admirably in a mission, even if it was a mission which had not even be focused on the extraordinary result which it had achieved.

Muldowney was justifiably elated.   He had discovered a plot

33

embellished with all the heady ingredients of a secret agent's most ardent desires. Gold bullion, a subverted army officer, and the possibility of corrupt powerful figures hovering in the background. Muldowney had by now completely discarded the element of uncertainty which had accompanied him since first dispatched upon his mission. Whatever trivial inquiry had been in Queally's mind when he had first sent his agent into the field must fade into total insignificance in the face of this truly remarkable coup.

Muldowney allowed himself to wallow a little longer in his glow of self approval. He had succeeded in completing a mission to which he had not even been assigned. He had secured a suspect who had not been previously identified or even sought, and had also recruited a fully fledged detective to back him up. Surely this was the ultimate in undercover ambition.

There was, however, now a more pressing problem than dwelling on the curiosities of Queally's operation and the men who served it. Something had to be done about the babbling army officer who had so unexpectedly delivered such astounding information. He certainly couldn't be left at large, nor could he be taken back to the police station for the rest of the night. Muldowney came up with a solution. His secret agent's rapid response system was functioning again.

"We'll hold him at the boarding house until the morning," he said to the detective. I'll get instructions about him then."

The detective was inclined to quibble. He had no authority to go back to the brothel and indeed his presence there at this stage could compromise the police raid, but Muldowney was adamant. There was no other solution. The policeman wanted to know why Muldowney couldn't get instructions immediately and set about transporting the prisoner to the Section's dungeons, but Muldowney evaded an answer.

He couldn't very well explain to a policeman whose service functioned twenty four hours a day that the nation's special security Section only operated from nine to five, and there was no way of getting in touch other than a fixed time call to his contact desk in office hours. To the best of his knowledge there were no facilities at all in the labrynthined corridors of the GPO for keeping prisoners. The disposal of the now highly sorrowful army officer was not going to be an easy problem to solve.

Muldowney, however, had underestimated Queally's resourcefulness. The call to Cronin at the appointed hour and a brief resume of the situation had resulted in a short delay while Cronin spoke to the Section head. Then came a peremptory summons back to headquarters.

"You're to come in quietly," Cronin warned him. "Don't let anyone see you and don't talk to anyone."

Muldowney swallowed the retort that the streets were full of people and up to a hundred minions of the postal service were likely to be around the building at any given time. The chances of getting unseen to the upper floor that housed the three or four rooms that constituted Queally's domain were pretty remote.

He could, however, obey the command of silence, realizing that in Queally's view such silence was in itself akin to invisibility. Indeed so totally disinterested in the doings of their fellow men were the denizens of the hallowed GPO that there was a very good chance indeed that Muldowny would get back unnoticed.

And so he did. Queally heard him out without comment. It was a truly remarkable tale. Muldowney delivered his narrative in hesitating tones from the usual standing position. As the end approached, Queally exhibited some very rare signs of perturbation. He stroked his chin repeatedly and opened and shut a drawer several times in succession without extracting anything.

"We shall have to take action," the Director said eventually.

Muldowney in a flash of sudden understanding realized that Queally didn't really know what to do. The omniscient head of the special department was flummoxed by the magnitude of his subordinate's discovery. Muldowney wondered if in fact for the first time in his career Queally had been faced with a really serious security issue. Had the Section head's long running spiderish regime really been fashioned out of webs of nonsense, Muldowney wondered disloyally.

He brought his wandering thoughts back to his chief as Queally cleared his throat, heralding a major decision.

"I'll have to take this to higher authority," Queally said.

For a moment Muldowney was surprised that there was indeed anyone higher than Queally. Then he remembered that after all both of them were civil servants, and in the civil service, no matter what one's sphere of influence there was always someone higher up.

"The army man," Queally said. "You'll have to get him to a safe house."

"Yes, sir," Muldowney answered. Queally nodded in dismissal.

"Where do I find a safe house, sir," Muldowney questioned in some alarm. His experiences of the past twenty four hours had made him vulnerable on the question of houses.

Queally thought for a moment.

36

"What's wrong with where you are at the moment," he asked.

Muldowney was momentarily stuck for words.

"It's a brothel, sir," he said eventually.

Queally nodded.

"Very good cover," he replied. "I trained you well."

Muldowney swallowed what he perceived to be the monstrous self delusion of his superior. Queally tapped the top of his desk with a pencil. It was, Muldowney knew, a sign of momentous intellectual activity, generally applied to cutting down the expence accounts of his underlings.

"The rest of the residents will be released today, sir," he explained. "There are quite a number of girls living there as well as the owners."

The spymaster exploded in a spate of moral indignation.

"They should be kept in jail," he stormed. "Letting people like that off with a few pounds of a fine is a waste of time and resources."

The penalty for plying the oldest profession was indeed a minimal one in the Irish justice system, fashioned on the basis that anything so draconian as a jail sentence might attract more attention to the evil pursuit than was necessary. Public morality dictated that the female half of such contracts must be chastised, but the public also had to be protected from any kind of salacious tittle tattle, and the very suggestion that there were prostitutes on the streets of Dublin or houses of assignation to be found within Dublin Corporation's area of remit was likely to undermine the whole fabric of society.

"Get hold of that detective again," Queally ordered. "Tell him to move in with the occupants, secure the premises and keep out any clients. Take Cronin with you to assist."

Muldowney nodded his assent, resisted the inclination to give a military salute, turned on his heel and left the office. He gave Cronin instructions to clear his desk and come along, grasping possessively at the whisp of power that had come his way with this sudden promotion over his erstwhile controller.

Cronin had not been brought into Queally's office to hear the undercover agent's report. This was an established Queally ploy, based on the belief that secrets were best maintained by ensuring that all reports were delivered verbally before being committed to writing. In this way, unsatisfactory aspects of a situation, which in some way perhaps might reflect on Queally's capabilities as head of Section, could be deleted from the record.

On this occasion, there had been no instructions to put pen to paper at all, a situation which Muldowney dutifully accepted. For his part, Cronin, well versed in the ways of command and decision making, acquiesced to his new role without demur.

Chapter Four

The plain girls arrived back at the house just before lunchtime. The morning court had gone its expected way. The usual petty fines were imposed and the silent Mr Conroy duly paid over the amounts in cash allowing the girls to be on their way. They arrived back more animated, more talkative than they had been in the sitting room the previous evening. Muldowney heard them crowding through the front door, laughing and pushing at each other to get in, adrenalin created by the events of the night evidently still not dispersed by the resumption of their more mundane daylight activities.

Muldowney was lying fully clothed on his bed, the colonel was locked in his room with Cronin sitting on a chair outside the door. The police detective had gone home to his wife and small children to catch up on his sleep. After a while the sounds of the girls below abated, there were footsteps on the stairs and along the corridor, bedroom doors were slammed and silence descended once again. The girls too were catching up on their lost night time hours.

Muldowney pondered the situation. The colonel had given them all the details of the operation that he knew. The secret agent was certain of that, but there were many missing links. The timing was only tentative, there were no names of the conspirators. Colonel O'Connor was adamant that his orders had come down through the military system. He had, however, been brought to a meeting with civilian officials as well. Soldiers and civilians shared the chain of command. The dominating issue was whether the soldier's tale was true, and if so was there a major conspiracy and how high did it go.

Colonel John Dominic O'Connor, a career soldier with twenty three years of service behind him, although a high enough ranking officer, could be no more than a minor player. He was a man obeying orders, and orders involving both staff officers and lower ranks had to follow an established chain of command. But those orders in particular had to start out from the civilian sector. The military could not originate the documents to authorize such a transaction. The colonel claimed that he knew instinctively that something was wrong, but was unwilling to pass his suspicions back up the officer command structure for fear of being accused of a breach of duty.

The more Muldowney thought it out then more he became convinced that there were very highly placed civilians involved. No one else could have access to the detailed sensitive information that was entailed. What did this mean. Were there powerful civil servants or perhaps even a member of the government directing the operation. There was also a nagging doubt. Was anything illegal really going on. What if the whole thing was a totally legitimate piece of state business and the addled colonel had got it wrong.

For a moment the very enormity of what he had let loose overcame Muldowney. His mind started to race over the ramifications which the plot provoked. Surely the whole affair was nothing more than the ravings of a man temporarily unhinged by the pressures of being arrested and disgraced.

At the same time, however, Muldowney believed with a cold certainty that the colonel's tale was true. O'Connor had spoken with all the authenticity that truth provides. Muldowny, almost at the outset of his career as a secret agent, had uncovered a conspiracy which men who served in secret all their lives rarely if ever encountered. He thought about Queally for a few moments. The spymaster had been inscrutable when the secret agent had recounted his tale. Had he had similar adventures as a young agent, Muldowney wondered. What sort of torrid conspiracies had been resolved to propel Queally to the position of head of Section.

Muldowney was elated at his success. He was imbued with

complete confidence that the conspirators would be trapped, the plot unraveled, and that his record would glow with the recounting of his brilliantly successful foray into the murky world of subversive crime. Muldowney was in reality a simple soul and had led a sheltered life. He had yet to encounter the viciousness which ambitious men invoked in the furtherance of their careers. He had no doubt at all that he would get all the credit that was due to him.

That Queally might present the affair in such a way that all the credit redounded to the spymaster did not occur to Muldowney at all. Queally, he felt sure, would tell the government exactly how well his brilliant agent had succeeded. Perhaps the story should not be told too exactly, he reflected after a moment or two. After all, the case had come about less by brilliant sleuthing than by the sheer chance of Muldowney's selection of a house of sexual commerce in which to reside on his first night undercover.

The red haired girl came to his room unasked, interrupting his thoughts. She was clam but perturbed. Her name, she said, was Veronica, an unlikely bestowal on one whose profession he now suspected was the same as that of the girls who had been in court that morning. It might be that she pursued a rather more profitable clientele. Muldowney certainly found her a great deal more appealing than the others.

Veronica's concerns were about the locked up army officer. The events of the previous night, even though she had apparently escaped the consequences simply by being out when the raid too place, had raised sufficient worries about further onslaughts by the police.

Muldowney decided to give her at least some insight into what was going on. He stopped short of producing his secret agent's card but carefully intimated that his was an official operation, fully sanctioned by the authorities, that he was in charge,   and that the imprisoning of a high ranking army officer in her house was only a temporary arrangement and that there would be no repercussions. Indeed, he hinted, a co-operative attitude on the part of the residents might lead to less police attention in the future.

She seemed satisfied at this and sat down on the edge of the bed, evidently prepared to chat and pass a few idle minutes. Muldowney warmed to her a little more. The heavy make-up of the previous evening was washed away, and she was paler. Her red hair was natural though, and she had tied it back to a braid, obviously her method of managing it in her off duty hours. She was older too, perhaps twenty eight or so.

Veronica was the first prostitute that Muldowney had encountered. The girls he had vaguely met in the house the previous night had not really made any impression on him. He had not been conscious of the fact of who and what they were until the arrival of the raiding party, and after that greater concerns had taken over.

The detective returned about half an hour later, interrupting their conversation. The girl got up to leave and Muldowney asked her to bring up some tea. She agreed and went out of the room. The detective shut the door carefully behind her. Muldowney swung his legs off the bed and looked at the policeman.

"We want you to work with us on this operation," Muldowney told the detective. "I've cleared it with my superiors."

The fact that the policeman's superiors had not given clearance of anything at all seemed of little consequence. The detective, his name was O'Brien, appeared suitably gratified at his involvement in such a momentous piece of undercover drama. It was on the back of such happenings that promotion surely came fast and furious. Previously modest ambitions of becoming a detective sergeant after a moderate passage of time were rapidly being replaced by visions of superintendent's rank and beyond.

Cronin came into the room at this point, bored by sitting with his by now morose prisoner. Muldowney made a perfunctory introduction. By now it was halfway through the afternoon and time for further action. Muldowney decided that a visit to the Central Bank was called for. Tea would have to wait. The three of them should go, he decided but this left the question of guarding the officer.

They went downstairs checking on the locked in prisoner on the way. Struck by an idea, Muldowney went to the kitchen at the back of the house, ignored a sullen Mrs Conroy who was busy with dishes at the sink, and drew the red haired girl into the corridor. He proposed to appoint her temporary guardian of the prisoner.

She agreed immediately and went upstairs to watch over the officer. Muldowney realised that he had successfully recruited a fourth member to his team. The question of credentials, qualifications, or indeed the approval of his superior did not arise. Firmly in charge of the operation, Muldowney in the back of his mind had decided that what he needed was experienced personnel. Both the detective and the prostitute were sufficiently well versed in the other side of life to equip them with them skills that were needed to deal with whatever might arise over the next few days.

The detective had brought a car, a miserable battered mechanical cohort of the local policing team, but Muldowney was glad of the bonus. He had vaguely considered getting around by taxi but knew that Queally's chastening and eliminating hand would immediately wipe out any claim for such an expense. The alternative would have been a bus to O'Connell street and a short walk to College Green where the

43

Bank was located, but fate had intervened in the form of a detective and his station car. Muldowney awarded himself more points for the special insight he applied to his recruitment policies.

They drove through the afternoon traffic, the detective putting a flashing blue light on the roof while Muldowney allowed himself to be swamped with a warming glow of earnestness and dedication as they dashed past the GPO and the Section head in his lair in the upper storey. Muldowney steadfastly kept his eyes front, resisting the temptation to glance up at Queally's window. Cronin was not so staunchly independent. He knew that fast cars and flashing lights were not apart of Queally's approach to affairs and he crouched down in the back seat stealing a quick furtive glance upwards as they dashed past.

They swung past the august frontage of the Bank of Ireland, once the parliament house of the bewigged and befogged, now housing the financial ascendancy of mid twentieth century Ireland. The eighteenth century aristos would certainly have envied the power of today's mandarins, but they had bartered their inheritance to Westminster and eventually been expunged from the scene.

There had of course been some erudite and democratic men amongst them, Muldowney reflected, but they had not prevailed and the days of their pocket boroughs had long gone. Now there was another ostensibly less autocratic parliament. Yet it too had its coterie of the powerful, the Grim Grey Men whose decisions were absolute.

A porter in a top hat and tailed coat was opening doors at the main entrance to the Bank of Ireland. He was a last sad remnant of the older order which had survived the mouldering of the broughams and carriages which had once swept up to the pillared portals of one of Dublin's most imposing buildings.

They were not, however, heading for this welcome from the top hatted flunkey. Their destination was a lesser building in a small enclave of a street alongside. The detective squeezed his car into a parking space and they got out. Muldowney nodded at Cronin and the big man knocked diffidently at the heavy closed door. There was no response. Muldowney pushed his colleague aside and hammered the panel with his fist. The door eventually swung open a foot or two, secured on the inside with a chain. A porter in a vastly more shabby uniform than the top hated impresario outside the Palladian bank alongside peered out.

Muldowney and the detective simultaneously thrust their respective IDs into his face and demanded entry. The porter hesitated a moment then reluctantly disengaged the chain. He opened the door just enough to allow them to filter in and closed it firmly again, securing bolts at its top and bottom and refastening the chain.

"I'll get someone," he said.

Evidently random visitors were not a regular feature of daily routine in this dimly lighted warren. This indeed was a much more powerful bank than the magnificent edifice next door, but one which obviously spurned any visible trappings of authority.

Yet in this rather mundane administrative building functioned the regulators of the Irish financial world. The top hated flunkey bowing and scraping in mock servility between the great pillars next door, and the hierarchy of financial decision makers which spiraled above him, all had to submit to whatever decisions were made by the occupants of this more insignificant adjoining building. This was the Central Bank, the regulatory authority of the nation's financial institutions.

Despite the production of their identification, it was a fairly lowly functionary who eventually arrived to deal with the visitors. Muldowney was irritated. He was gradually assuming a much more haughty role and manner, one which befitted his position as head of mission. His team and its authority was now three investigators, plus their newly recruited jailer on duty back with their temporary prisoner. Muldowney had become a powerful man. Hesitating, uncertain, quibbling clerks, such as this one reminded him too acutely of his own very recent low grade past.

He told their welcomer abruptly that someone higher up would have to deal with them on an urgent issue of national importance and motioned the official back the way he had come. Muldowney and his companions followed without invitation. They went along a short passage and up a flight of stairs. Their guide paused once or twice outside impressive paneled doors which evidently concealed a series of personages of increasing importance and finally after some perturbed consideration, knocked on a selected door and was called inside.

Muldowney introduced his party generally as members of the secret service and having asked their guide to leave, got down to explaining the reasons for their visit to the man behind the desk.

John Rodgers was second in command at the Central Bank deferring only in power and function to the Governor himself. He was an administrator, a glorified if somewhat better paid civil servant than the usual departmental habitué. Immediately Muldowney saw that he was dealing with a companion spirit.

One bureaucrat was much like another when it came to coping with issues outside the normal run of affairs. They generally didn't want to hear, certainly didn't want to take action, and were absolutely determined that nothing of a disturbing nature which might cause repercussions should be brought to the notice of their superiors.

Muldowney's administrative stint in Social Welfare had honed his manipulative skills. He got around the banker's defenses, laid the urgencies of the situation very firmly upon him, and eventually got access to the vaults below.

The deputy governor led them downstairs, through a security door and into the basement. A heavy iron door with a triple locking system barred their way. It was opened by the drab porter who had followed in their wake. There were no windows and in response to an irritable command from Rodgers, the porter switched on the lights.

The banker crossed hurriedly to the center of the room where a green cloth covered what at first glance appeared to be a small bench of table. He pulled the cloth away and there exposed and glistening dully was a neatly arranged pile of yellow ingots which Muldowney already knew were gold. The banker lifted one and handed it to the secret agent. It was heavy, tapered to the top, the underneath was stamped with a crest and a number.

"This consignment is ready to be moved," the banker said. "We don't normally keep bullion more than a few days in this vault, but we had to get ready to make the shipment."

Muldowney nodded. The others were silent, evidently overcome by the sudden reality of encountering a fortune. Muldowney, however was less impressed. He was totally immersed in the logistics of his situation. The gold was here. It was going to be moved and it was going to be stolen. That was the kernel of the tale told by the sexually adventurous colonel. However, the issue of its value also impinged on his thoughts. He posed the question.

"Just over a million," the banker replied.

Cronin whistled softly. The detective drew a deep breath. Muldowney, the banker and the porter evinced no outward sign whatever.

Muldowney began to prise out the details of the transaction. The banker pointed to a small hand operated lift at the back of the vault. There were two small trolleys nearby.

"We bring the bars up in the lift," the banker said, "and wheel them out to the security van at the front door. It will take twenty trolley loads to move the consignment," he added, proud of his grasp of mathematical detail involved in dividing a ton of gold into manageable trolley loads.

The destination was the Bank of England, the departure date was two days ahead. Muldowney replaced the ingot, looked at his hands involuntarily to see did any speck of gold stick to his palms – it didn't – and motioned the party out of the vault. They returned to the banker's office. Muldowney sat in silence for a few minutes, going over the situation in his mind.

"The current arrangements will stand," he said finally to the banker. "I will travel in the security van. My colleagues will follow behind."

The banker was worried now. The prospect of losing the gold, even after it had left the protection of the bank, was something which could cast a permanent blight on his future prospects.

"I will have to inform the Governor," Rodgers said. He allowed his hand to hover over a phone. Muldowney shook his head.

"No one else must know," he said firmly. "Security on the matter is essential.   We don't know how big this thing is, or who exactly is involved. We are quite satisfied about your status," he assured the banker rapidly and untruthfully. "We had you checked out before we came."

There was an implication here that other employees of the bank might be under suspicion, even the Governor himself might be compromised, but his deputy let it pass. The enormity of the whole affair overshadowed any clear analysis of the situation and its implications.

"Are you sure about all this," the banker asked again. "The documents are totally in order." He had the glorified clerk's blind reliance on the power and authority of signed pieces of paper.

Muldowney repeated his assurances. "We are certain," he said.

In fact, of course, neither he nor Queally back in his lair had fully checked out the possibility of error. Facts, in Queally's manual, should never hinder the progress of a good investigation. It was possible that the whole thing was sheer fantasy. Muldowney dismissed the niggling doubt. The banker had asked another question.

"How can you be sure that the consignment will be safe," Rodgers asked. He studiously avoided any reference to the word 'gold' perhaps guided by a bureaucrats's reluctance to deal with anything other than paper based facts and data.

"We have our own plan of campaign," Muldowney said cryptically. "We are going to catch these people red handed and the only way we can do that is when they make their move. We'll arrest them as soon as that occurs," he added confidently.

His colleagues made no contribution to the conversation, assuming that whatever Muldowney was saying was in fact the cut and dried plan already laid down by Queally in consultation with the wider security service. They had no indication that Muldowney was in fact off on a solo run, planning an operation which he had yet to properly formulate and making decisions which rightly lay with the Director in the confines of his special department.

"Nothing will happen before Thursday," Muldowney assured the banker as they took their leave. "Just carry on as normal, take the usual precautions with regard to security and tell no one that we have been here. We'll be back on Thursday morning and join up with the army escort when it arrives."

He held out his hand to the now well shaken and only slightly reassured banker and led his colleagues out of the office. They went silently down the stairs and out to the car. Even though all three of them had been fully aware of the implications of the operation in which they were deployed, the confrontation with the gold in the security of its vault had a chastening effect. Even Muldowney felt simmerings of awe tinged with a slowly fomenting concern about the seriousness of the affair to which they were committed.

He decided to get back to Queally and instructed the detective to drop them in O'Connell street, far enough away from the GPO to prevent him from learning just where the Section had its base. Despite the new comradeship that was being forged with the detective, the over-riding discipline of secrecy instilled by Queally ruled. No outsider must know where their headquarters was. He sent the detective back to the boarding house to relieve Veronica as custodian of the woebegone army officer whose lustful temptations had brought the whole affair to light, and followed by his silent colleague, walked up the street to face his master.

Chapter Five

Muldowney left Cronin in the outside office and went boldly into Queally's sanctum to report. He was already a much more confident operative, his mental attitude honed from the effects of the remarkable development of his mission. He recited his report to the spymaster quickly and without any ornamentation. There was no need, the tale in its own right was one which could stand quite adequately on its own.

Queally heard him out in silence and then swung his swivel chair around to stare out of the window. Muldowney said nothing, waiting for his chief to digest the information. After a moment or two, Queally turned around again to his subordinate. Muldowney fancied that he was even paler than usual and certainly his voice was lower, the usual abrasive hectoring tone of a man running out of patience with his underlings was absent.

"What have you got in mind" the spymaster asked quietly.

Muldowney took the question as a sign of his rapid progression in the estimation of the Section head. He gave a brief outline of the plan which he had proposed to the banker. He would travel in the security van with the bullion. The others would follow behind the escort. At some point, he believed, the convoy would be attacked, the soldiers would be ready, and the raiders would be captured. As he outlined his plan to Queally he became more and more conscious of the fact that it was a very flimsy strategy indeed.

They could be going blindly into a situation from which it might be very difficult to extricate themselves if they met up with superior force. However, it was unlikely that amateurs would be able to overcome trained soldiers. There was still the haunting doubt at the back of his mind. Was the thing real. They only had O'Connor's word to back up this plot to steal the bullion.

51

Queally turned it over in his mind, thought for quite a long time, and finally imparted some of his deliberations to his subordinate.

"I think we should make a dummy run," he said. "Make up a shipment of fake bullion. If anything goes wrong and we lose it, at least we will still have the real gold."

Muldowney agreed. It was a sensible precaution. He admired the spymaster's capacity for such a decision.

"We shall have to prevent any word about the switch from getting out," he said. "It will have to be done inside the bank vault and only senior staff will be able to know anything about it."

Queally made his decision.

"You, Cronin and the policeman must handle this yourselves. Only the deputy governor Rodgers is to be told. I leave the details to you."

Dismissed, Muldowney returned to the outer office, collected Cronin and headed for the street. This time he had no compunction about relaxing some of the constraints of the department's pursestrings and hailed a taxi. He gave his colleague a brief resume of Queally's instructions.

The taxi brought them back to the boarding house and they went upstairs to the soldier's room. He was still secure. The girl was sitting beside the bed, reading. O'Connor himself lay on top of it, his hands folded behind his head.

He jumped up when the secret agents came into the room, but Muldowney motioned him back down again. The army officer was obviously about to launch a protest at his continued captivity, but a glance from Muldowney silenced him immediately. The secret agent had acquired an even more visible mantle of command. He was rising to the pressures of leading his small team towards successfully foiling the conspiracy. His senses were fine tuned. A much more assertive manner in place. The studied mildness of the disinterested civil servant who once had adjudicated on the trivial misdemeanours of the unfortunates who tried to extract unentitled benefits from Social Welfare had vanished. This was a new more positive, more decisive Muldowney, one who was hourly growing into the full dimension of his secret agent's role.

Queally would have approved in a limited sort of way. His underling was rapidly becoming a kind of clone of the Director himself. Had he been present to see what was happening, the spymaster would have laced his approval with the imposition of controls to ensure that this, and indeed any other lower ranking agent in his service, would not aspire to too much authority and independence.

But here, unknown to the spymaster, it was all happening. Had he been present with the agents and their prisoner in the bedroom at that moment, Queally would have felt more than a twinge of unease. Mudlowney was beginning to shape and mould events even further. It was not an attitude and approach that the spymaster would endorse. Watching and reporting were the duties of Queally's men. Decision making was not part of that process. Seldom, indeed, perhaps never before, had an agent in the field functioned in such a strong decision making mode.

"We are gong to let you go now," Muldowney told the solider who could hardly contain his relief at the announcement. Once again he started to rise from the bed but the agent put a hand to his chest and pushed him back down again.

"I want to make it quite clear to you," he warned ponderously. "You are being released on licence. You are to report for duty and follow your orders and escort the bullion."

He paused for a moment and then shot what he hoped was an unexpected question to the soldier.

"Are you sure you've told us everything."

His voice had all the menace applied during the officer's first interrogation and O'Connor disintegrated again. He shook his head violently in denial of having any further information. He knew nothing more. He was to command the escort and sign the aircraft manifest. He would be monitored by radio. That was all he knew.

Muldowney studied him for a few moments and then, satisfied that he had been told the truth, waved the officer to his feet.

"Remember this," he commanded. "If you say anything to anyone about your arrest and contact with us you face a court martial and twenty years or more in jail."

The officer shuddered, wiped his forehead with his now much crumpled pale green handkerchief and straightened his uniform. Cronin handed him his cap from a dressing table. O'Connor put it on, straightened it by the peak and gave a half salute.

"What do I do if there is a change of plan," he asked.

Muldowney thought about this for a second or two. It was a valid point. They had to keep in touch. He eyed the girl speculatively.

"Take the number here," he said. "Telephone Veronica with whatever information you have. In fact," he went on deciding

54

that there should be a much more tangible contact system, "you are to make a call to her every six hours, between now and the time you leave the barracks."

The girl started to object but was silent in the face of Muldowney's authoritarian glance.

"You are to stay here until this is over," he told her. "We'll ring in periodically to see if there have been any developments. You'll be paid for your time," he added suddenly conscious of the fact that the red haired girl might suffer some loss of earnings over the next forty eight hours. It was unlikely, however, that the Section's rate of pay for part time work would measure up to the remuneration which she normally received for her services.

The army officer left and Muldowney replaced him on top of the bed. He stared at the ceiling for a long time. Cronin sat down and offered the girl a cigarette. She lit up and both of them focused upon the recumbent head of mission.

Muldowney shared his thoughts at last. He had been grappling with the problem of providing a credible substitute for the gold bars. Queally had insisted on a dummy consignment. He had no suggestion and confessed as much to his companions. The girl blew smoke down her nose and resolved the problem almost immediately.

"Heavy brass," she said. "It could be made up in bars to look like gold."

Muldowney looked at her with a growing degree of fondness.

"Brass ingots," he said. "Yes, it could work alright. But how are we going to get such things."

The girl had the answer too.

"There's a brass works across the river," she said. "Up near the brewery. They could make up the bars to any shape you want."

Muldowney and his fellow agent exchanged approving glances. It was a credible option. Once more Mudlowney felt a flash of congratulatory self approval for his acumen in deciding to enroll such an obviously talented recruit.

The detective, O'Brien, arrived at the boarding house a short time later and they filled him in on the details of the substitution plan.

"We'd better move on it then," the policeman said. "If we don't catch the foundrymen before they close for the day we'll be under a lot of pressure in the morning."

They piled into the detective's car leaving the girl behind to monitor the brothel phone. It was unlikely that there would be an early call from the colonel but the first of the fixed time checks would be due in a few hours time and she would have to be there to take it.

They reached the foundry just before it closed for the night. The arrival of the small detachment of agents, backed by the authority of their special passes, succeeded in holding back the foreman and a couple of workers and within minutes the fires were at full flame again. The foreman ladled molten brass into moulds and they were racked up to cool. Two hours later the job was done. Muldowney looked approvingly at the steaming ingots for a few moments and arranged to collect them the following morning.

"We'll need a truck," Cronin observed as they left the grimy building, their clothes drenched with sweat from the heat of the fires. Muldowney's hair had been singed slightly when once he had got too close to the flames, and the detective was nursing a minor burn which he had received when he had inadvertently put his hand on a still warm piece of metal.

Muldowney knew how to get a truck. He directed the detective to drive them down to the Posts and Telegraphs central garage and evicting the gateman from his tiny office, dialed security. There was a relationship between the postal snoopers and Queally's Section. Their roles often interchanged. Special transport arrangements for surveillance purposes and telephone tapping were often on the agenda. There were other unspecified services available from time to time as well, Queally had hinted when briefing him during the early days of his enlistment.

The arrangements for a truck to move the brass ingots were put in hand without question. They could pick it up the next morning as soon as they were ready. No questions would be asked by the staff on duty. It was a pretty standard routine. With such detachment and ingrained efficiency did Posts and Telegraphs provide regular and ongoing facilities for covert activities mounted by the various wings of state security.

Muldowney slept at the boarding house. It was quiet. Evidently normal business had been suspended while the unwanted residents were around. Cronin and the detective went home. They met next morning for an early breakfast in Bewleys Grafton street café. Cronin wolfed his toast and coffee appreciatively, the detective was a more steady eater. Muldowney limited himself to a cup of tea and idly pushed the sugar bowl around the marble slab which served as a table top. He wasn't hungry and anyway it was too early to sample one of the sticky buns for which the Quaker confectionery business had been renowned for over a century.

They collected their dingy green truck with its postal logo on the sides without incident.   The brass bars were loaded by the hands at the foundry and they drove back to College Green. Their next stop was the bank. They backed the truck up to the doorway and after a few words with Rodgers, trolleys were organised to bring the fake bullion inside. All other bank staff were banned from the hallway and vault areas while the brass ingots were unloaded. Muldowney dragooned a passing uniformed policeman to keep curious members of the public at bay while the consignment was being brought into the building.

The unloading work over and with two covered piles of ingots now standing in the vault, they went upstairs to Rodgers' office. The deputy governor decided that this was an occasion when the habits of a lifetime could be relaxed and some libation offered to persons other than good old boys from subservient financial institutions. He produced a bottle of Jameson and glasses and poured a measure for each of them.

Muldowny lay back in his chair and mused over the sequence of events. Cronin rang the boarding house and checked with Veronica. The fixed time calls were still coming from O'Connor. There were no developments. The escort arrangements for the bullion still stood.

The banker cleared his throat. He seemed nervous.

"There is a slight problem," he said. "We still have to ship out the gold. It can't be delayed. Our Reserves are under pressure. The bank of England is very insistent that we top up our national deposit. It is imperative for the interests of the State that it arrives in London on time."

Muldowney pondered this new aspect of the situation. He had not planned to take the gold out of the bank at all. He totally accepted the banker's comment about the pressures on the State. It was not for Muldowney to question the methods of securing the country's financial stability. If gold bullion had to be moved it had to be moved. It was the secret agent's business to see that it was moved in safety.

The banker's insistence, however had made things more complicated. Taking the gold out of the bank was risky, even with the dummy shipment. Just how big a risk was involved? Surely they would be able to foil the plot without any prospect at all of losing the buillion.

He turned the problem over in his mind and finally solved it in the most straightforward way possible. Both consignments would travel to the airport, but the real gold would be moved in the postal truck which would stay close to the military vehicles but far enough apart to escape a raid if that occurred. His colleagues would also be near enough to assist Muldowney when had had to arrest the robbers.

Muldowney dismissed any need for further back-up. He was certain that the gold would be taken by some sort of trick and not by force of arms. The whole point of O'Connor being enrolled as a plotter was to ensure a quiet undramatic transfer of the bullion. The colonel hadn't been fully briefed yet but Muldowney was satisfied that the robbery would be accomplished by an apparently fully authorized handover of the bullion to another group of soldiers or indeed even civilians. The success of the heist depended entirely on O'Connor being in command and giving the orders to his men as if they were on normal duty.

Confident now that he had worked out the routine, Muldowney gave his instructions to his subordinates.

"We travel behind the escort," the detective queried. "Not with the convoy itself?"

"Yes," Muldowney answered. "Postal trucks are almost

invisible. No one will pay any attention to you and you will be able to keep the convoy under surveillance as well as guard the gold. I will travel in the army truck with the fake bullion as arranged."

He kept the rest of his thoughts on the intricacies of the plot to himself. The guideline of the secret agent's management agenda was once again in play. The need to know rule was being applied.

They were at the bank well before the arrival of the soldiers the next morning. The real gold was loaded into the postal trck and the fake ingots put into the soldier's vehicle when it arrived. The point of embarkation for the consignment was the military airfield at Baldonnel, only a few miles beyond the city. Muldowney settled himself in the military vehicles, his presence authorized but unexplained to the soldiers by their commanding officer. O'Connor had kept religiously to the fixed time call agenda through the night, confirmed the departure and arrival times of the convoy at the bank and at the airfield, but had no further information. His masters had not been in touch. The details of whatever was going to happen had not been passed down the chain of command.

Muldowney was satisfied that the officer was telling the truth. No one had been in touch. He didn't know how the gold was to be seized. The soldier was calmer than he had been at any time since his arrest but was still nervous. He had all the hallmarks of a man who knew he was in trouble but did not fully grasp the enormity of his peril.

Muldowney peered out through an eye slit in the back curtain of the truck. He could see the post office vehicle about a quarter of a mile back, travelling independently. Two army personnel carriers and an armoured car rolled on immediately behind his own truck. The brass ingots were piled neatly on pallets besides him. Muldowney sat back satisfied, all self doubt banished now that the mission was under way.

He remained calm for most of the journey form the centre of the city, through Inchicore village and down the main road towards Baldonnel. It was only when the convoy in fact turned into the side road which marked the last stage of their journey that he became alarmed. Nothing out of place had occurred. There had been no stop, no attempt to delay the convoy, no indication of anything unusual which looked like a threat to the consignment. It now seemed as if the entire journey to the airfield was going to be accomplished without incident. And so indeed it proved to be the case.

The convoy turned into the airfield gateway, halted for a few moments to allow the sentries to inspect the colonel's papers and was then waved through. Minutes later they had pulled up beside a camouflaged nissen but on the edge of the tarmac. Muldowney dropped quickly out of the truck and went up to O'Connor who had traveled in the leading jeep.

The officer shrugged his shoulders. He was evidently as flummoxed as the secret agent.

"Perhaps it was called off," he said. "I don't know."

Muldowney turned to look for the post office truck. It was held up by the sentries at the gate. Without written orders they couldn't get in. O'Connor sent a sergeant across to get them through and a few seconds later the green postal service vehicle was parked alongside its military comrades.

"What are the arrangements," Muldowney asked O'Connor.

It was quite obvious that nothing was going to happen on the base. The place was swarming with redcaps and soldiers, all well armed and clearly capable of coping without any untowards episode. O'Connor consulted his file of papers.

"A plane is due in from London in half an hour," he said. "We load it up and it flies out again immediately."

Muldowney's early buoyancy and sense of purposeful accomplishment had collapsed. There was to be no dramatic rescue of the nation's treasure, no arrest of high ranking and highly placed conspirators. In fact there was nothing at all to justify the whole operation, which it now seemed had been built on the ramblings of a discomfited soldier caught in circumstances far from befitting an officer and a gentleman.

Muldowney looked closely at the colonel. It was apparent, however, that he was just as mystified as the secret agent. He had been expecting something to happen. He was part of something sinister, and yet even though he was a key man, the plot seemed to have been abandoned without giving him any briefing whatsoever. Muldowney was devastated. His big chance had evaporated into thin air. What had gone wrong? Somehow there must have been a leak. The conspirators had learned that they had been rumbled and called off the heist!

Just to satisfy themselves that everything was in fact going to be completed without incident, Muldowney and his team waited while the bullion was loaded. The members of the escort party were slightly bemused when they found themselves unloading the gold from a non military vehicle which was not even a part of their convoy, but quietly applauded their officer's vigilance when it became apparent that there were two different consignments. The brass ingots were transferred from the army truck back into the postal lorry and when the plane was trundling down the runaway, the now dejected Muldowney and his colleagues climbed in and drove towards the gate.

The full extent of the collapse of his mission took hold of Muldowney. Instead of returning as a conquering hero, he was returning as the butt of what was not even a practical joke but a highly coloured fiasco which would require a great deal of defending. Queally would have a field day. The castigation of his unfortunate subordinate would reach unparalleled heights.

Requisitions would have to be signed to pay for the brass ingots, for the use of the postal service vehicle, explanations would have to be given for the usurping of the detective O'Brien from his duties, and there was the question of his own and Cronin's input of hours. How could he justify the promised remuneration due to the red headed girl who had acted as the soldier's temporary jailer. It was all a complete and utter disaster. Muldowney was as yet too naïve and inexperienced in the ways and wiles of the secret service to realize that disasters were part and parcel of the service's very existence. No one ever knew that such incidents ever occurred because they became secrets themselves. In such a manner did the Section and more importantly its Director survive.

Cronin broke into his reverie.

"What do we do with this stuff?"

He jerked his head towards the back of the truck where the pile of brass bars lay under their concealing blanket.

"We'll dump them somewhere," Muldowney replied absently.

He was still pondering the ramifications of the events of the day. What was it all about. He puzzled over things all the way back to the city to no avail. There was just no solution to the enigma. He was still convinced that there had been a plot. He was more certain than ever that the army officer had been telling the truth. But what had gone wrong. Why had the project been aborted. Had O'Connor given them away. The agent was sure that there would have been no other leak. The only point of contact with the conspiracy had been the soldier. Therefore only he could have been the source of alarm.

They were back at the boarding house with the questions rolling around in Muldowney's head still unanswered. The detective parked outside the front door and they went inside. The girl met them in the hallway. There was more colour in her cheeks now and her previous almost overdone air of self control had been replaced by an obvious buzz of excitement.

"The colonel has just been on," she said. "The gold has been taken. It didn't get to the English bank. He got a call telling him well done."

Muldowney almost broke down, but managed to get a grip on himself. The girl repeated the message. His brain wrestled frantically with this unwelcome news. He had no way of checking whether the message was true or not, but he knew instinctively that the girl had got it right. The gold was gone. His mission had been subverted and destroyed. The reason for the lack of action during the transport of the bullion became clear. There was never any question of an armed raid. The procedure was much more sophisticated.

How was it done? He puzzled for a long time before arriving at the answer. The shipment had been redirected. If it had not arrived at the London bank it had been sent somewhere else. The paperwork was the key. Phony documents, organized through official channels had been used. Someone somewhere had pulled off a remarkable coup, got away with a million in gold and he, Muldowney, star of Queally's Section, had helped them. The conspirators were waiting for the gold to fall into their hands even as Muldowney was escorting it to the airport.

The others stared at their pale and crestfallen leader. They had not yet grasped the implications and complexities of the red haired girl's information. Muldowney wiped away a layer of sweat from his forehead that threatened to pour down over his eyes.

"We've been had," he said weakly. "They've got away with it, right under our noses."

The girl opened the sitting room door and they went inside, slumping into chairs to ponder Muldowney's words. The other three were totally confused. Muldowney, whitefaced, shaking, beat his fists on the arms of his chair in exasperation.

The detective was the first to make a move.

"I've got to get back on duty," he said flatly rising to his feet.

It was true but it also gave him an excuse to put some distance between himself and what was now quite obviously a promotion affecting disaster.

"You can get in touch with me later."

Once he had gone, Cronin spoke across the room to Muldowney.

"You had better get on to Queally," he said. "If you're right and they've got the gold, there will have to be some sort of high level action."

Muldowney said nothing for a few minutes, slowly going over the sequence of events, from the first moments of the officer's interrogation after the police raid, through the discussions with the spymaster and their visit to the bank. He wondered about Rodgers for awhile. The banker had to be in on it, he decided finally, slapping his hand on his knee in a gesture which welcomed a sudden flash of revealed truth. O'Connor was enrolled because he would have traveling custody of the gold's shipping papers. The soldier had concealed that factor, despite the pressure that he had been put under.

"Rodgers had to be a part of it," he told the others decisively.

"It couldn't have been done without him."

Cronin and the girl stared at him in silence.

"They needed a man in the bank," Muldowney explained. "If the consignment was being redirected the paper work had to be cleared. Whoever dealt with the transaction in the bank would have caught on to anything out of the way unless he was part of the operation. The same thing applied to O'Connor. He was in charge of the paperwork as far as the airport. That's why they needed him."

He made a snap decision. Reporting to Queally could wait. With the detective absent they were short a man, but the girl was there and available. He gave her a quick description of the banker.

"Go down to the bank and wait outside," he said. "When Rodgers comes out follow him, use a taxi if you have to but keep him under observation. I want to know where he goes and who he sees."

The girl got up to go and Cronin intervened again.

"We'll have to get the postal truck back to the garage," he said. "There'll be a howl for it if we don't. I only got it out for twenty four hours and it's needed for mail duties."

Muldowney nodded his agreement. The Section's relationships with post office security was not one which should be compromised by over stretching their arrangements.

"Dump the brass bars off somewhere," he instructed his colleague. "There are plenty of places, old building sites, something like that and bring the truck back."

He looked at his watch.

"I'll wait here for Veronica to call in and we'll meet up later."

The still sullen Mrs Conroy made him some tea and he went to his room, still feverishly battling with the conflicting thoughts and emotions which the events of the morning had induced. He dozed fitfully as the hours passed. Veronica still had not called in. Cronin hadn't been back either, and he was beginning to suffer the first pressures of panic when the boarding house owner called him to the phone. It wasn't the red haired girl, however, but the detective, back in his city centre stallion and on duty.

"I thought I'd better let you know," he said. "Veronica has been arrested. She's here in the station in the cells. She was picked up outside the bank."

Muldowney cursed. The detective picked it up over the telephone.

"It's not what you think," he said. "She wasn't pulled in for soliciting. The Special Branch took her in. She's being interrogated by blokes from headquarters."

No explanation was needed about the muscle of the officers who now had Veronica in custody. The country's most powerful and feared detectives were in the Special Branch. For a moment Muldowney felt chilled and worried. Some very heavy firepower was coming to bear on his investigation. He put down the telephone and returned to his room. He had a quick wash and shave and changed his shirt. Then it was down the stairs and out into the street. There was still no sign of Cronin returning but Muldowney knew what he had to do. Matters had got out of hand. It was time to report to Queally.

He walked quickly down Capel street and turned up Mary street to the brighter lights of the city centre. A newsboy was calling a late evening edition at the corner. His raucous cries

67

were shouts of defiance against the imperious outlook of the mighty newspaper offices a few feet away. The *Evening Herald* staff had gone home too early. It was the *Evening Mail*, the rival paper for real Dubliners which had rushed out a special edition to report a late in the day city drama. Someone had been found dead on a disused site near the Liberties. The body was lying across what looked like piles of gold bars, but a suspicious officer had scratched one with a nail and they had been identified as brass.

Muldowney was sick in his stomach. He stopped momentarily at a street bollard and leaning across it retched fruitlessly for a second or two. He turned into O'Connell street and ran the last few yard towards the side door of the general post office building.

He pulled up in his tracks. Something unusual was happening. A group of uniformed policemen accompanied by two men in civilian clothes were grouped outside. The plain clothes men had their hands permanently in their pockets and Muldowney recognized them for what they were, armed Special branch officers.

He knew instinctively that now was not the time to go into the office. Something was terribly wrong. He must go back. The police were there to arrest him, he was certain. He turned and melted into the crowds of evening shoppers. Now he was faced with a real test of his abilities. The undercover secret agent who had embarked so confidently on his secret mission less than three days ago was now dependent on going undercover, not to discover secret crimes, but to survive. Muldowney the secret agent was on the run. In the classic phrase the hunter was now the hunted.

Chapter Six

The Grim Grey Men of the National Security Committee sat across the table from Queally as he made his report. He had gone to the Cabinet room in a state of extreme concern. For the first few hours following the departure of the bullion plane from Baldonnel he had looked forward with total confidence that as usual he would receive the customary sparse commendantion that generally followed his briefings. But the Security Committee had other news.

It was not in Queally's nature to allow himself to be overcome by events, but on this occasion he was almost completely shattered by the dramatic and devastating twist in the bullion situation. Muldowney had not been able to report in so he had not known the gold was missing. The Grim Grey Men had got their information about the disappearing bullion directly from the Central Bank. The Police Commissioner had been brought in. Queally was caught out. He had believed that all was well and he had made up his file accordingly. Everyone knew about the gold being missing except the head of Section who was in charge of it.

Now his unit was under investigation. His men were suspects in the affair and he, the state's senior security man, was instructed to submit to a Special Branch inquiry. He had no option but to name Muldowney as the senior agent in the field, and had sat fuming in his office as the police moved to capture his operative in the street.

Muldowney had not intended to keep Queally in the dark, but the cordon of police outside his office had cut him off from his superior. Queally had given up Muldowney because he had come under unaccustomed pressure. The spymaster was adamant that his agents were clean and only doing their job. That, the Commissioner had told him bleakly, remained to be seen.

Queally knew that his section was in serious jeopardy. He was being threatened in an unprecedented way by the Commissioner whose force he despised as a band of uniformed unintelligent traffic wardens. It was not normally Queally's way to submit to such pressure. The spymaster's vanity did not allow for any kind of denigration by rival services to go without redress. The Commissioner might head a force of thousands but Queally ran the senior service. Nonetheless he was in trouble. The fact that his agent was an out of touch wanted man had cut the spymaster off from an scraps of information that Muldowney might have picked up.

Now Queally tried to be casual, to give the lie to any suggestion that his affairs were in total disarray. The Grim Grey Men, normally five in all, but with the addition of Finance minister Malachy Finucane on this occasion, stared at him sternly and without any semblance of pity or concern. Queally momentarily floundered for words and finally got off an expression of disbelief about the disappearance of the gold.

"My operatives were present when the bullion was loaded," he declaimed desperately. "I know that the gold was put on the plane. My responsibility ended there."

The Chairman of the Security Committee interrupted him unsympathetically.

"The gold should never have been allowed to leave the country," he said. "You missed out on the whole thing. Your operatives escorted a shipment which was being stolen from the moment it left the Central Bank. Your own security was a smokescreen for the conspirators."

Queally was silent. His mind raced over the senior minister's statement. He sensed the implications immediately. The Chairman gave an approving nod as he saw that Queally was taking the situation on board. The spymaster's response,

70

however, was not exactly what he had expected.

"This was a plot engineered from quite high up, in the civil service, in the bank perhaps, or indeed even by a member of the government itself," Queally offered combatively.

He had independently come to the same conclusion as Muldowney. All the known facts pointed this way. The Chairman was not impressed. He considered Queally's comment for a moment, however, and allowed his expression turn to one of disdain as he surveyed the recalcitrant spymaster.

"That is total nonsense," he said. "Your intelligence is obviously very low grade. You have been totally outwitted on this occasion. You spent your time going after very small fry in the affair. You went after the feet whereas you should have been pursuing the head."

"We had no way of progressing any further." Queally made an attempt at explanation. "Our army contact himself didn't know who his principals were. He got his orders down the line."

"You should have moved on him and traced the whole thing along. And above all you should have stopped the shipment," the Chairman rejoined sharply.

This was a plain enough indictment of incompetence. In vain Queally tried to explain that they had manufactured a dummy shipment to ensure that the real gold would get through. The Grim Grey Men were having none of it. They had also got a grip on the fact that the kernel of the plot lay in the subverting of the legitimate arrangements to export the gold. This was where the Section had slipped up. As matters stood Queally and his men had opened the doors and allowed the bullion to be spirited away.

The Justice minister spoke up.

"There are two issues which are to be dealt with right away," he specified. "The first is to find out what happened to the gold when it arrived in England and then trace it down. The second is the murder."

"Murder," Queally echoed. "What murder?"

The Grim Grey Men looked at him with barely concealed contempt. Their manner said everything to Queally. Here was a man who was quite obviously not on top of his job.

Quietly the Chairman related the contents of the police reports which had reached him before the meeting. A murdered man had been found lying across the brass ingots manufactured and dumped by Queally's department. The spymaster had glanced idly at the report in the paper the previous evening but had failed to link it with the matter in hand. There was indeed no reason why he should.

He sank down in his chair, a rapidly shrinking shadow of the concerned but still smug self satisfied head of Section who had entered the Cabinet room a few minutes before.

"The Special Branch have arrested your man, Cronin," the Chairman went on. "He was seen leaving the scene in a postal service vehicle and we traced him through the department's own security section. He admits dumping the brass bars. These were his instructions, but he claims that he met no one and knows nothing about the body. He can be released on your authority but obviously he's a prime suspect."

Queally digested this further piece of calamitous news in a growingly disturbed state. He was rapidly losing control of the situation. The intervention by the police in any aspect of his Section's activities was totally unheard of. He was more than

72

clear about what might well be the result. His career could be in shreds, his days as head of Section numbered, his future prospects negligible.

The Chairman spoke on, his clipped and harsh tones breaking through Queally's personal review of his circumstances.

"We can only assume that your Section itself was penetrated as part of the conspiracy," he said. "Your man Muldowney is obviously the weak link. The success of this conspiracy is down to him, possibly with Cronin as an accomplice. It is quite on the cards," he added, "that both your agents are involved in this."

"We want Muldowney found," the Chairman spoke again. "He has got to be caught right away."

His voice rose slightly, his tones more harsh.

"You are responsible, Queallly. It was your unit that was in charge. We want these people caught, and we want the country's bullion back."

His grey colleagues nodded in agreement. Queally picked his file up from the table and rolled it up. It was a sign of his perturbation. In the spymaster's normal orderly controlled existence files were kept flat, their contents were briefly worded pristine sheets, carrying minimal information which would seldom if ever be scrutinized by anyone other than himself. He put it down on the table again and it slowly uncurled. The eyes of the men across the table momentarily followed its progress.

Queally regained a degree of self control and began speaking in as measured tones as he could muster.

"I shall need full authority," he said. "If this conspiracy points to members of the government I shall have to question everyone in the Cabinet, ministers of state, and all the senior staff in their departments. I shall begin interviews immediately, starting in Finance for obvious reasons," he said, suddenly becoming more confident, his eyes repaidly surveying the assembled ministers.

The Finance minister, Malachy Finucane, was silent. He was not a member of the Security Committee but was at the meeting because of his responsibility for the consignment. He had been instructed by the government to initiate the transfer of the bullion. Queally who had expected a protest from Finucane was immediately suspicious. The other Grey Men expressed surprise at his proposal.

"Question ministers," one of them echoed. "The whole idea is preposterous."

Queally shook his head, his resolve stiffening and a degree of control returning.

"I shall have to investigate this at the highest level," he said. "The bank and the army will have to be looked at as well. There are many sides to this. What is the money needed for? Is there a plot to overthrow the government?"

He threw out this suggestion recklessly without any forethought whatsoever, but he felt that he needed to extract some revenge for the contemptuous manner in which he had been treated by the committee up to now. It was the turn of the Grim Grey Men to be uncomfortable. There was a long silence.

Finally the senior minister spoke again.

"You believe that someone is trying to bring down the government?"

Queally shrugged.

"It is a logical question in the light of the disappearance of the bullion," he said. "Ordinary criminals could not undertake such a difficult and risky operation. In any event they would not have the official contacts necessary to set it up."

The Grim Grey Men looked at each other uneasily.

"Very well," the Chairman decided. "You have full authorization to do as you must. But I must make it quite plain," he added, "this has got to be wrapped up quickly and securely. Speed is of the essence. There are to be no leakages to the press. That man Muldowney is to be caught today. Do I make myself clear?"

Queally stood up.

"Yes, sir," he answered briskly, scooped up his file and left the room.

He went immediately back to his office and put the machinery in motion to have Cronin released. The big man arrived in the office an hour later, white faced and obviously severely shaken. He had spent several hours being cross examined by detectives about the body found with the brass ingots. He had been only reluctantly released.

Cronin recounted his actions of the previous evening. There had been no problems while he was at the wasteground with the truck. He threw out the bars into the weeds and drove away. He had been at home when the detectives came to arrest him for questioning in the early hours of the morning.

"We've got to find Muldowney," Queally stressed. "Did he have anything to do with the body?"

Cronin shook his head.

"I don't see how," he said. "He didn't know where I was going to unload the bars. I just hit on the place as I was driving around."

Queally dismissed the obtrusive corpse from his deliberations for the moment and turned his thoughts to Muldowney.

"He might go back to the boarding house," Cronin suggested. "Or he might ring in again."

Queally's fruitless thoughts turned in another direction.

"This girl, how does she fit into things," he demanded.

Cronin had little information on Veronica either. As far as he knew Muldowney had recruited her to keep an eye on O'Connor when they had him locked up and to answer the phone when the officer was making his fixed time calls later on.

Exasperated Queally threw down his pen and sent his underling back to the outer office. He needed time to think this out. He closed his eyes and unconsciously rocked backwards and forwards as he provoked his brain into motion. There were three strands of action which could be taken, he decided. The army connection through O'Connor, the Bank through the deputy governor, and the Cabinet itself as he had provocatively suggested at the Security Committee meeting. He had relished that moment. The sting in his words had given him some small sweet sense of revenge for the humiliation he had undergone earlier at the meeting. He decided to leave the Grey Men and their colleagues alone for the moment. It would be too difficult and take up too many man hours to interview every member of the government at this stage, to say nothing of their staff.

It was conceivable, however, that the chain of command leading down to the military escort commander, O'Connor, might yield some further clues involving other officers, but on the face of things he decided that the banker Rodgers was the best immediate bet.

Half an hour later he was in the Central Bank building off College Green. Rodgers had not risen to become second in command of the country's financial regulatory authority by cracking under pressure and whatever alarm he had at first displayed, the banker now had his feelings well under control. He met Queally in his office, extended a limp hand and sat back to listen to what the intelligence chief had to say.

Queally probed as deeply as possible but only elicited fairly basic information. The decision to move the bullion had been taken by the Cabinet as part of a support move for the Irish currency. The transaction was authorized by the Minister for Finance. The members of the Security Committee were also members of the Cabinet and were aware of the decisions in the ordinary course of business.

There was nothing particularly unusual about the transaction. Bullion was not moved very often, the banker admitted, but he had overseen the dispatch of several consignments of varying value in the course of his career. The destination was the Bank of England's Threadneedle street vaults in London, but it had never arrived. The bullion had been loaded into an aircraft and vanished.

Queally mentally upbraided himself for not having sent his team across the water with the consignment, but the whole thrust of Muldowney's reports had been focused on the staging of some kind of operation on this side of the Irish sea. It was a reasonable assumption that once the gold had been loaded onto the aircraft at Baldonnel it was safe.

Queally watched the banker closely as he put his questions. There was nothing here to indicate any kind of collusion with the underworld figures or anyone else. Eventually the spymaster came to the conclusion that Rodgers was clean, although nervous. At the same time Queally felt that he wasn't being told the whole truth. But his visit had yielded one item of useful information. He had got the name of the senior civil servant who was the link between the bank and the Department of Finance. He went in search of the official.

Eamon Dalton was a principal officer at the Department of Finance and as such had evidently taken a lot of systematically channeled abuse from even more senior mandarins by the time Queally got to his office. The bullion had been requisitioned on the authorization of the Finance Minister, he told the spymaster icily. The minister would have got his instructions from the Cabinet, he went on. Dalton himself had drawn up the documentation. The decision was minuted, implemented, filed and totally above board, he assured his interrogator. If something had gone wrong it had done so outside the scope and responsibility of the Department.

Queally blinked at him through his glasses.

"The only problem I have with what you tell me, Mr Dalton," he said, "is that the Security Committee have themselves told me that they do not rule out a conspiracy at the highest level. A million pounds worth of gold has been stolen in circumstances which point to very senior officials being involved. Perhaps even you," he added maliciously.

Dalton met his eye steadily enough.

"The Minister has instructed me to carry out a full enquiry within the Department," he told the spymaster. "I have already done this and I am satisfied that no one here was in anyway involved in the affair. The paperwork was handled only by

78

myself and the Minister, Mr Finucane, who signed it, and of course, the typist," he added. "It was sent by official messenger in a sealed envelope to the bank. There was some telephone discussion about the arrangements," he went on. "I didn't think it was necessary to actually go down to the bank myself."

Queally was tempted to observe that the care of a million pounds worth of gold bullion called for some more hands on management than a telephone call. He said nothing, however, civil servants were bred to take the easy way out. He himself would favour the view that a senior man need not walk if he could use the telephone. He realized that he was up against a brick wall and left. On the face of things there was very little more he could do in the Department. Everything seemed to be above board, yet his questing intuition told him that someone high in the civil service or in the Executive held the key that would unlock the mystery.

He returned to his office and sent for Cronin again. The big man had nothing to report. Muldowney had not been seen and had not been in touch. The police had not yet released the red haired girl. The spymaster asked about the murder investigation.

"I rang one of the blokes in the murder squad," Cronin replied. "They don't know who it is. The post mortem puts him at around forty. He had soft hands – probably was some sort of office worker and he was strangled."

Queally looked at his subordinate's hands. They were large farming hands, befitting a man who came from the land and who had once put in his working day in the Department of Agriculture. They were well capable of either grappling with an unruly bullock or choking the life out of a human being. He dismissed the thought. Cronin was not as far as he knew a violent man, anything but, and there was nothing dramatic

79

about his manner and personality that would link him with violence in any way. But Queally knew that deep down, the urges that drove men to work in the obscure and furtive ways of the secret service would also encompass a disposition to violence once the comfortable shell of conventional behaviour had been shattered.

He sent the agent back to the front office and closed his eyes to think again. Only one over-riding thought came to the fore. Muldowney! Muldowney was the key. He had to be found, and found quickly. He lifted the telephone and spoke to an assistant police commissioner at Dublin Castle. Muldowney's status as a fugitive was reinforced but this time he was also the country's most wanted man. For Queally it was a reluctant decision, but the Security Committee had given the order, and the spymaster too had questions to ask his missing agent.

Chapter Seven

Muldowney had never felt so lonely or so depressed. Suddenly, inexplicably, his world had been blown apart. Despite his surveillance and precautions, the bullion had apparently been whisked away, his unauthorized female associate had been arrested, a body which might or might not be Cronin had been found with the brass ingots, and Special branch and uniformed officers were on guard outside his office.

He made several phone calls to the Section, but could not get through. He tried to get Queally on his private line as well, but the spymaster was apparently also out and there was no reply. The uncertainty tore through Muldowney. Was it Cronin who had been found dead with the brass ingots. If so who had killed him. What devil's twist had taken over this mission. Were the police looking for him for murder. Was he right to have fled when he saw them grouped outside the post office building the previous evening.

The morning paper on the bar gave very little further information about the dead man and the brass ingots, and of course, there was no mention at all of the stolen bullion. This was one secret that was never likely to become emblazoned across the columns of the newspapers. Exasperated he tried to get Queally one more time and went back to the quiet corner of the dockside bar in which he had taken refuge.

Muldowney had spent the previous night in a doorway along the quays, and when the bitter wind which swept up river found him out, moved into the comparative shelter of a telephone kiosk. It was less draughty but just as cold. The first light of dawn brought little relief but remembering his experience near the cattle market, he had walked the docks area until he eventually an open early morning public house. It was dirtier, rougher and less patronized than the cattlemen's hostelry, but it was warm and the barman served him up a hot whiskey without question. A half dozen or so burly dockers were downing their breakfast pints, and outside he could hear the start up cranking of the machinery as the port got ready for the day.

He whiled away another hour or so, read the paper and sucked up the heat from the fire. Then after another fruitless call to the office, reluctantly left the shelter of his haven. It was raining again and the river smelled badly. He walked towards O'Connell Bridge, past the magnificent Custom House and the shabby link with the days of Labour leaders Connolly and Larkin that was Liberty Hall. Muldowney reflected in passing that it was time the building was replaced with a more modern depiction of trade union muscle. Muldowney despite his profession was a firm believer in the right to organize.

He turned down a side street towards the fire gutted shell of the Abbey Theatre, finally finishing up beside Clery's,. the cheap century old Irish version of the great London department stores. He slipped in through a side entrance and aimlessly walked the floors until he finally decided upon a front window vantage point from which he could stare across the street to the GPO.

He had a good view both of the Henry street side entrance to the building and of Queally's shuttered office window high above the pillared portico at the front. The police had gone from the doorway although there was no way of knowing whether they might have a presence inside. Anyway if they were after him Muldowney had no doubt that Queally would hand him over. And yet, he pondered further, he might not. If there was any advantage in keeping his subordinate out of the hands of the police, Queally would have no compunction about doing so.

He stayed in place for an hour or more. The store was already busy, the counters packed high with piles of linen, blankets, clothes and household ware. Single men from the country, families, overweight mothers brooding over possible bargains, priests, walked by totally absorbed, checking Denis Guiney's prices against their household lists. Overhead the money cups in their pneumatic tubes shot backwards and forwards from the counters to the cashiers.

Muldowney had no plan in mind. His decision in coming to the store had been a half conscious one, hoping that he might perhaps somehow update himself on what had occurred. It was coming up to midday now, and the Section would empty its tiny workforce into the street for a quick hard pressed hour of frugal sustenance taken at the cheapest of the surrounding cafes. Only the spymaster would remain at his desk. Hopefully, he would catch a glimpse of one of his colleagues, Cronin even, if in fact it was not his body which had been found the previous evening. His patience was eventually rewarded. Cronin was alive. The big man came through the doorway, and walking the few yards into O'Connell street, turned towards the Liffey end.

Muldowney trailed his quarry from his side of the street. Cronin passed the Metropole and Easton's bookshop, and walked on until he reached the last building on the Bachelors Walk corner. It was one of the new rash of Italian ice cream parlours that had followed Cafolla's brash foray into the capital city's main street. Cronin went upstairs where the younger duffle coated people congregated and Muldowney could see him through the wall of glass panes that made up the front of the building, first at the counter and then sitting at a formica topped table. A half moon sign in the colours of the rainbow depicted the restaurants name – the Rainbow Café - on the exterior of the façade.

Muldowney was sitting opposite him at the table before the big man was even aware of the fact that he was there.

"Christ" he exploded, spilling his thin over milked coffee over a half eaten sandwich when he suddenly realised just who had joined him.

Muldowney shot a hand across the table and seized his wrist.

"What the hell is going on," he whispered fiercely. "I thought that you had been murdered. The police were outside the office when I went back yesterday afternoon."

Cronin wiped his lips with the back of his hand and then put both hands up to his head in a gesture of total dejection. He seemed to be a man pushed almost to the edge.

"This thing is out of hand," he said. "They're looking for you. They think that you killed the bloke. I know that you didn't" he interrupted himself. "I brought the brass bars to the site. You didn't know where I left them off. Queally will give you up if you go in."

"Who was killed," Muldowney demanded. "Why?"

Cronin shrugged his shoulders.

"I don't know. Nobody knows."

He was half tearful, his voice rising and the people at the nearest table looked at them curiously. This was a man, Muldowney decided, who had come under much more pressure than himself.

"Tell me what happened," Muldowney urged.

The other was silent for a moment.

"I picked out this place to dump the brass, left the truck back to the postal service garage and went home. The police pulled

84

me out of bed. They let me go this morning and I reported in."

Muldowney was flummoxed.

"Who is the dead man," he demanded again.

Cronin made no reply.

"There's hell to pay about the gold," he said eventually. "Queally has been to the government. They're going to fry him, and I hope they do so," he added with a sudden surge of bitter relish.

Muldowney closed his eyes, suddenly tired.

"You'd better buy something," Cronin remarked. "That manageress is on the prowl."

The stern lady who ruled the Rainbow café for her Italian masters was notorious for her determination to ensure that very customer spent his due and left as soon as he had eaten his repast. A girl came by clearing tables and Muldowney ordered a coffee and a couple of cakes.

They were cheap, sickening, garishly coloured confections, far removed from the wholesome fare on offer in his favourite haunt, Bewleys Oriental Cafe on Westmoreland street, just across the river. He pushed his thoughts about the cool and tranquil old fashioned Quaker restaurant out of his mind.

"We have got to get this cleared up," he said urgently, desperately casting for explanations. He looked at the big man. Cronin had nothing to offer.

"Queally says that you were in on the plan to steal the gold," Cronin said finally. "He reckons that the bloke who was killed was part of it and that you did him in and dumped the body

85

there. He says the dead man had to be shut up for some reason.

"I didn't even know where you were going to drop off the brass," Muldowney responded absently. "I don't understand it."

"I told him that," Cronin said.

They both thought it over for a few minutes without result.

Cronin finally shifted in his chair.

"I have to get back," he said. "The police are gong to question me again, and I have to be around."

Muldowney nodded.

"I'm going to work on this from the outside," he said. I need the army man O'Connor's address. He's the only connection I have."

He firmed up his plan in his mind.

"Go back to the office and see can you get O'Connor's address for me," he ordered. "I'll wait here until you come back. You can make some excuse to come out again."

Grateful for being dismissed the big man paid his bill and hurried out. Muldowney sat for a few moments and then he too got up and left. The instinct for survival was becoming more cultivated. He crossed the street and stood behind a circular continental street urinal that some city father in his wisdom had persuaded the Corporation to install as a piece of functional street furniture. Sure enough a few minutes later a black police car drew up outside the café and four detectives got out and rushed upstairs.

Muldowney stepped into the crowd gathered at a crossing point and crossed the street with them. He knew where he stood now. He was on his own. Cronin would give him up to the spymaster and Queally would hand him on again.

A curtain of bitter black despair enveloped the secret agent once again as he slowly walked back along the quays. His mood now was so sombre, so self destructive, that he didn't bother to keep himself concealed in the crowd, not even keeping an eye out for an patrolling uniformed officers.

He climbed the steps into Amiens street station and sat down for a while on one of the wooden seats that an ostensibly caring railway line provided for its passengers traveling northwards. For a moment he was tempted to buy a ticket and leave the state on the Enterprise express, but he immediately discarded the idea. He knew nothing of the Six Counties or England. Whatever chance he had of surviving this crisis, he would have to do it on familiar ground.

It was one thing to try to lose himself in the suburbs or down the country, it was quite another to flee the state altogether, but even as he was mentally processing and discarding these thoughts, he was alerting himself once more to the immediate need of avoiding not just the uniformed police but the Special branch and other state security agents that he was sure were already searching for him. He had to hide, but how and where.

He had very little money left from the office float that he had drawn when he first set out on his undercover mission. A handful of coins and a ten pound note was the total amount of cash that he could muster. There was enough to keep him in food for a day or two, but not enough to pay for any kind of a roof over his head as well.

He shivered in the coldness of the draughty station and pulling up his collar against the chill walked back down into the street. He needed a shave and a night in the open in his clothes had left him dirty and uncomfortable. It was getting dark now and the street lights were on, matching the headlights of the increasing flow of evening traffic as the car owning citizens headed homewards. The less affluent majority queued patiently at bus stops or rushed for suburban trains. Muldowney felt lonely and miserable. He walked across Butt bridge, found his way to Westland Row and out towards the more prosperous suburbs of Ballsbridge.

Here was a different world, a world of old wealthy Dublin families, living sedately in tree lined avenues with pristine parks, tennis courts, cricket grounds and rugby pitches. He had passed the ornate iron railings of the Royal Dublin Society's elegant showgrounds, a mecca for the world's international showjumping stars, and horse proud Anglo Irish landowners, when a bus stopped on the far side of the street and disgorged its complement of urgent passengers.

Most of them headed back across the bridge to the less affluent side of the Dodder, but one or two walked on towards Shrewsbury road, where wealthy merchant families lived cheek by jowl with eminent surgeons and ambassadors from important countries. There was a familiar figure amongst the disembarked commuters, striding along with a crisp military bearing, although in civilian clothes. Muldowney recognized the army officer immediately. His erstwhile prisoner and author of his misfortunes was walking only yards ahead of him, totally oblivious to the fact that once more, by sheer chance, he had crossed the path of the secret agent.

Muldowney held back, now totally alert, tense and concentrating like a retriever pointing and waiting for the word of command. He followed the soldier from a safe distance using all his sleuthing skills to make sure that his quarry remained unaware of the fact that he had acquired a tail. Muldowney was a determined man. It was this officer who had deliberately withheld the vital information about the re-direction of the bullion that had caused so much trouble for the secret agent.

O'Connor wasn't quite sure of his destination. He checked the brass plates on the railings of various houses, each time resuming his brisk walk up the wide and gracious avenue. Somehow he had apparently regained the bearing and confidence which one expected to find in an officer. Eventually he halted again, checked the plate on a gate and turned into one of the small gardens that provided access to the elegant mansions that lined the roadway.

A flag hung limply from a sort mast and there was an armorial plaque on the front door. Muldowney was too far away to distinguish either the colours on the crumpled flag or the script on the plaque, but he had no doubt that O'Connor had arrived at an embassy. He was standing at the top of the flight of wide stone steps now, waiting for someone to let him in. A beam of light shot out as the door opened and after a few moments of conversation the army officer went inside and the door closed behind him.

Cautiously Muldowney crossed the street and walked up to identify the building. As he had correctly surmised it was an embassy. He walked on and hid himself in the shadow of some shrubs that formed one of the gardens and communed with himself for a moment. The army officer had gone into the German embassy. What had brought him there?

Muldowney stayed at his vantage point for at least another half an hour. Then a big American Studebaker drew up outside the embassy and he stiffened to attention. The car didn't impress him. It was a Dublin taxi. Dublin favoured big flamboyant noisy imported American motors for its taxi trade. The more status conscious private owners drove the better makes of English cars, Rovers and Triumphs, the smaller man had his Cork assembled Ford. There were those, of course, who could afford a Jaguar, and a select minority who favoured a Bentley or a Rolls Royce.

The officer came down the steps, carrying a small hold all this time, and got into the taxi. Behind him in the lighted doorway Muldowney could see a tall foreign looking man in the classic German officer mould, thin, bespectacled, but with the unmistakable bearing that beclaimed a much more impressive military pedigree than that of his Irish counterpart. The taxi drove off, the embassy door was closed, and Muldowney unable to mount a pursuit, was left to meander idly along once more, worrying thoughtfully about this sudden new development.

What did it mean. What was the connection. There was no doubt in his mind that O'Connor's visit to the embassy was linked with the bullion business and therefore with his own dire predicament. But he was wary now. Unexpectedly but with the little bit of luck that every intelligence man needs, he had come into possession of a new scrap of information. Suddenly he had something more to bargain with, something with which he could put some pressure on Queally to extricate him from the dire situation which diligence and a sense of duty had put him in.

He rang Queally and this time got through to the spymaster right away.

"I have some new information," he told the Section head. "We have to meet."

He shot down Queally's immediate suggestion that he should go to the office.

"You know as well as I do that the police are looking for me," he said sharply. "You put them on to me. I don't know what the full story is but I know that my best chance at the moment is to stay on the outside."

The spymaster took a moment to consider his options.

"What do you propose," he asked cautiously.

"I want a briefing," Muldowney answered. "I need to know just what is going on from your side and then I'll let you know what I have."

The spymaster considered matters again for a few moments. He realized that he needed Muldowney and he was certain that despite what appearances might imply, his absconding agent was loyal and also the only lead he had. Whether he was part of the conspiracy or not was in fact irrelevant. Muldowney had information. He was a source, and in fact at the moment he was Queally's only source. For this reason alone, Queally decided, he would have to keep him out of the hands of the police. There was a chance that he could get the agent back under control even on the outside. It was worth the risk if Muldowney could come up with the information that would allow the spymaster to get on top of the whole affair.

He came to a decision.

"Stay undercover," he ordered. "We'll have an outside meet if you won't come here. You can pick the place. Make it somewhere as inconspicuous as possible."

Muldowney already had a meeting place in mind.

"The Black Horse outside Inchicore," he said. It's on the canal. It's quiet there and there won't be too many people around." Queally agreed and they fixed a time a couple of hours later.

Muldowney headed back towards the city gain. He reached the canal and set off towards the country end, passing Portobello and the old canal hotel where the barges once set down occasional paying passengers who traveled with the coal and corn. There were little hump backed stone bridges crossing the waterway at intervals along his route. Black and white painted lockgates raised and lowered the water levels to allow the barges to progress all the way down to Ringsend Basin.

He felt safe in the darkness. There was only an occasional street light along the canal bank. He had allowed himself a couple of hours to complete the several miles walk to the pub on the canal bank, right beside Inchicore Bridge. The Black Horse was a watering hole for working men, a slightly rural haven on the outskirts of the city, yet within easy reach of the sprawling new suburbs which housed inner city Dubliners who had been transported from their homes by the Corporation. He took a quick look inside just to make sure that Queally had not sent an advance party to take him.

It was too early yet for the late evening regulars. The after work drinkers had gone home and the only customers were a heavily built raucous drunk with missing front teeth and a small slight man with a moustache. They were both evidently painters, their overalls were dotted with multicoloured splashes. Two bicycles propped against the wall outside with ladders and cans of paint tied to the cross bars convinced Muldowney that they were exactly that.

There was something familiar about the bigger man, who appeared to be the most imbibed of the two, but Muldowney didn't know his crony at all. He nodded at the barman, warmed himself at the fire for a moment or two and then went back outside. He decided that his best position was where he could see the spymaster arrive and make sure that he came alone.

THE IRISH SECET AGENT

Queally came walking up from the village a few minutes before the appointed time. He had evidently taken a bus and got off opposite the church, deciding perhaps that he too should approach with a degree of caution.

Muldowney gave the spymaster a few minutes to settle down in the pub and went cautiously inside. The painters were still at the bar, the bigger man was poring over come handwritten sheets of paper, from which he read out a few lines every couple of minutes. Both he and his crony and the barman ignored him. Queally was sitting in one corner surveying him with a look of marked distaste on his face.

He greeted the agent irritably and jerked his head at the two inebriates on the far side of the room.

"Are they with you" he asked suspiciously, concerned that Muldowney might have recruited even more unauthorized and unsatisfactory personnel.

Surprised Muldowney looked at the pair again. The bigger man was reading laboriously from his sheets in a vowelised Dublin accent. The delivery might have been uncouth but there was a lilt and rhythm and contented possessiveness to the words that convinced Muldowney that the painter had written them himself.

"Why would you think they were with me," Muldowney asked his chief, surprise in his voice.

Queally grunted.

"Brendan Behan is one of the boys. He has done his time in Mountjoy. I thought perhaps he was involved in this."

Muldowney looked at the objects of Queally's suspicions.

93

"They're painters," he said slowly.

Queally nodded.

"Yeah. The little bloke is from the country. He does a bit of signwriting. They do some of the shops around the town, and houses as well."

"They're not with me," Muldowney said firmly. "I know nothing abut them. I picked this place because it is out of the way. They just happened to be here."

Queally was satisfied.

"What have you got to tell me," he demanded.

He made no effort to buy Muldowney a drink and the secret agent made no offer either. The barman well versed in the ways of customers made no move towards them. He knew immediately when people wanted to talk privately and when they were there purely for a pint.

Muldowney told the spymaster about his unexpected encounter with O'Connor and his visit to the German embassy. Queally took in the information in silence.

"He left with a bag," Muldowney ended. "It had to be a payoff."

Queally considered his subordinate's report. He had no doubt that Muldowney was telling the truth. His agent was not really capable of deep dissembling and Queally knew it.

The spymaster took Muldowney through the whole sequence of events again, from the first encounter with the red haired girl and her directions to the brothel, through the bullion delivery and finally once more to the episode outside the

German embassy.

"It's a puzzle," he commented finally. "I can see where most of it fits together, but there are loose ends. And one of them is this body which was found with the brass bars. Who is this man and who killed him?"

Muldowney was as perplexed as the Section head.

"I didn't know where Cronin was going to dump the brass," he said. "There was no pre-arranged place for it. Perhaps the dead man is a different business altogether. He might just have been left there A coincidence perhaps."

Queally didn't believe in coincidences.

"This murder is connected,' he said. "We just haven't worked it out yet."

He looked at the disheveled agent.

"You're a mess," he said. "Get yourself cleaned up. You'll attract attention."

"I'm to stay on the job then," Muldowney asked, relief in is voice that at least he still had the authority of the Section behind him.

"I can't help you with the police for the moment," Queally said. "The Special Branch are out after you as well as the uniformed men, but as far as I am concerned you're on active duty."

He brought out a notebook and pulled out a page.

"This is where O'Connor lives," he said writing down an address. "It's just outside the city. He's the best lead we've got. In fact" he corrected himself "he's the only lead. It looks as if the bullion may have wound up in German hands, and O'Connor is the linkman. Keep him under observation," Queally ordered, "and report in by telephone if you have any further information."

Muldowney raised the plight of the red haired girl. Veronica's arrest had been one of the more disturbing aspects of the case up until the time that he had spotted the police waiting for him out side the Section office. Queally refused to discuss the girl.

"She's still under arrest," he said. "We disown her entirely. You know the rules."

The spymaster got up and left without any further admonition. He had accomplished his mission. His agent was back on the leash again and would stay hidden. Queally now had a hidden watching eye on a prime suspect who could well lead them on to greater prizes. He was more than satisfied. The operation was onward bound and he was certain that his department was as close as it could get to the action. That he was defying the instructions of the Security Committee by abandoning the plan to have Muldowney arrested caused him no concern. His personal intelligence needs far outweighed the orders of the Executive.

Muldowney, reluctant to leave the warmth of the pub, listened to the declaiming Brendan for a few more minutes. Then conscious of the fact that Queally could still be double crossing him and that he could be picked up at any moment, walked out into the night air.

He decided that there was little point in trying to get out to Rathfarnham, a village several miles outside the city and trying to find O'Connor's home in the dark. He should have demanded some cash from Queally, he reflected ruefully, but the spymaster, always parsimonious, would probably have told him to send in a docket to accounts totally ignoring the practicalities of such a procedure.

The next move was to get a place for the night. His dirty, unshaven and rumpled appearance, as Queally had pointed out, would make him very noticeable. There were, however, other people who lived in Dublin, whose circumstances did not allow them to be as dress conscious or indeed as clean as the more conforming citizens.

He walked back towards the city, and when he reached James's street and the invigorating healthy smell of the brewery he turned down a hill towards the Liffey. It was getting late enough now and he hurried on, trying to catch up with another vagrant who was shuffling along a few hundred yards ahead of him. Muldowney knew instinctively that he had to be heading for shelter, and sure enough, he turned into the austere official building which called itself an Institute for mendicants. A side door was open, the light from inside flooding out and Muldowney followed the derelict inside. He halted beside him at a hatch. They were both to get a bed for the night.

"You're in luck," the official grunted at him when his turn came. "There's one bed left. Write your name in the book and put down your work and your last address."

It was officialdom's idea of grapping with the problem of homelessness by trying to attach some form of classification to those who had neither work nor homes.

Muldowney wrote down a fictitious name and address and handed back the stubby pencil.

"There's bread and cocoa in the day room," the custodian said. "Your bed is the last one in the first dormitory upstairs."

Obediently Muldowney went in search of the humble supper which the institute offered the city's homeless and downed a mug of hot unsweetened watery cocoa and a doorstep of thinly buttered bred. It was as welcome as a full dinner in the Gresham hotel, he decided. He climbed the stone steps to the next floor and found his bed. There were forty beds lined up along both sides of the dormitory. Everyone one of them was occupied, many of the lost and tired already snoring in a fitful sleep that gave some relief from the turmoils of a destructive daytime existence.

He lay down in his clothes and pulled a threadbare blanket over himself. He found it hard to sleep with the snoring and coughing and cries that periodically rose from the collection of wasted humanity that sheltered there. His own mind was in turmoil, but he took some comfort from the fact that he was officially back in action. He attempted some personal re-assurance. His deprived surroundings were part of being undercover, yet another facet of a secret agent's secret life.

Chapter Eight

Muldowney was on the street before eight o'clock the following morning. The rules of the Mendicity Institute were resolute. A night time's minimal succour would be provided, nothing more, and the destitute would not be permitted to stay one minute beyond breakfast time. The pack of squalid humanity that had slept there overnight was driven out and the door closed firmly behind them. The breakfast fare had been rough but wholesome enough, a sausage and a slice of bacon, with a couple of slices of bread and mugs of bitter black tea.

His unknown comrades fanned out across the city, making their way to retreats that only they knew of and which would harbour them during their daylight hours. Muldowney walked briskly along the river towards the city center. He had been able to wash and shave and the night's rest and the cleanup had done wonders for his physical comfort and general morale. He got a bus beside O'Connell bridge and within half an hour was walking up a country lane.

He had to ask directions twice, but eventually he came to the soldier's house. Its name was painted on a white washed gate pillar. The house itself was set back with a short drive running between two small fields to the front door. A grey horse and a bay pony grazed contentedly in one of them.

It was a pleasantly peaceful scene. A whitewashed country house set in a rambling untidy country garden with mature trees and clusters of shrubs and some daffodils already starting to bloom in the early spring. Muldowney walked up the road a few yards and sat on a stretch of dry stone wall to work out his next move. He was at a serious disadvantage. This wasn't the city where he could follow a quarry with the intervening crowd providing cover. Here was open countryside. One lone man could not fallow another lone man undetected. There was another problem. If the officer left by car,   the agent would be left behind.

Even as he came to these conclusions an army car came up the road, a uniformed driver at the wheel. It swung into the driveway and came to a halt at the front door. The horse and pony in the field, startled, cantered around for a moment or two, then settled again and put their heads down once more. Muldowney went as close to the gateway as he dared, caught a glimpse of O'Connor stepping into the car, then turned his back and bent down to tie a shoelace in the time honoured method of disinterest as the car swung out again and headed off towards the city. Once again Muldowney had lost his man.

He stayed where he was for a few moments, weighing up is moves. His target had gone, but was probably destined for the Curragh Camp or one of the big city barracks. However, since this was definitely his home, he was going to come back at some stage. His absence gave an opportunity to reconnoitre and perhaps get some insight into his itinerary and whatever else might be found inside the house.

A straightforward course of action seemed best. He walked boldly up to the front door and knocked. There was no response so he went around the back and came to a sagging wooden door leading to narrow enclosed verandah that ran along the back of the building. A small boy came out to greet him.

"My mother's upstairs," the boy piped. "What do you want?"

"I've come to see Colonel O'Connor," Muldowney said. "Can I come in."

"I'll get my mother."

He returned a few minutes later.

THE IRISH SECRET AGENT

"You can come in. She'll be down in a minute."

He waited, conscious of the fact that he presented a distinctly errant appearance. The woman – he assumed it was the soldier's wife – was looking at him suspiciously, and he explained his rumpled state by saying that he had just come off the boat from England. He showed her his official card briefly to allay any suspicions she might have had about this early morning interloper and gratefully accepted an invitation to rest up for a few hours until her husband's return. O'Connor had left no information about his destination. There was apparently nothing unusual about this, but she thought he would be back in the early afternoon.

Muldowney studied her for a moment. She was a pleasant active kind of woman, very much a country village type, he decided, and her house had the feel of well matured comfort. She brought him into the front room and stood silhouetted against the morning light stream through the French windows for a few moments. She was a lot younger than her husband and her figure had obviously befitted from her riding interests. There were photographs of horses and family members on hors on the mantelpiece and on the piano and around the room.

It was when she moved away from the window and across the floor that he saw the fading mark of a substantial bruise on her left cheek. She caught his glance and reddened slightly but made no comment and then left the room to make some tea.

The boy came in and sat down on one of the chintz covered arm chairs and started to quiz the visitor in the casual carefree manner that children of his age often adopted. When he got older he would probably be sulky and spotted, but at present he was a fresh faced talkative youngster, his attention for the moment taken with the unexpected caller.

Muldowney hedged a bit when the boy asked whether he was in the army with his father.

"You must be a lower rank," the boy remarked candidly. "You're much younger."

I'm in a different regiment," he said to get himself out of range.

The boy's mother came back into the room with tea and biscuits on a tray. Muldowney and the boy fell silent. The agent took the tea gratefully and studied the woman again. She was indeed a good deal younger than the colonel, but she looked tired, a little bit more worn than her years. She had heavy black shadows under her eyes. She had put some powder over the bruise and it was not quite as noticeable. She caught his scrutiny and immediately guessed his thoughts.

"The horse hit me in the face," she said in explanation.

The boy looked at her sharply and said nothing. All three of them knew it was a lie.

"I have to go out," the woman said after a while. "I won't be long. Declan will keep you entertained, I'm sure."

Then struck by the realization that he had said he had crossed from England on the boat, she asked if he would like to lie down upstairs. Muldowney thanked her but rejected the offer. He felt that it was better that he should be alert when the colonel returned.

"I'll stay down here, if you don't mind. I won't put you to any trouble."

She left the room and a few minutes later he saw her pushing a bicycle down the short avenue to the road.   The boy started to chatter again. He wasn't at school because of a cold, but he was going back the following day, he confided. Then with the curiosity of children he asked to see Muldowney's official pass. He had been clinging to his mother when the agent had produced it the first time. Reluctantly Muldowney brought it out again and let the boy look at it briefly. He was obviously disappointed. There was nothing at all exciting about the limp piece of stained pulpboard and few lines of print. His father's badges and ribbons were much more stimulating.

Muldowney felt a need to upgrade himself.

"I'm in Intelligence," he offered.

The boy's eyes widened.

"You're a spy," he exclaimed.

The agent nodded non committally.

"Something like that."

Now the boy had a hundred questions, most of which turned on whether or not his father was part of Muldowney's intelligence network. Mollified by the sudden and unexpected elevation of himself in his young admirer's eyes, Muldowney embellished his story a little more. He decided to mention the German diplomat in a bid to see whether the boy knew of any connection.

"I'm working with your father on a special project," he said. "With our government and the German government."

"You work for Germany as well," the boy questioned excitedly, the naming of one of the warring foreign powers of the previous decade raising all sports of expectations. Muldowney hedged again.

"In a way," he said, and tried to change the conversation.

But the boy was having none of it. Suddenly adventure had touched him, far outweighing the edge which being the son of a soldier had given him over the boys at school.

Pressed hard by his youthful and exuberant companion Muldowney spun a few imaginary tales likely to in some way satisfy the insatiable appetite of a fired up small boy until eventually his companion tired of the subject and wandered out of the room. Relieved Muldowney slipped off his shoes and put his feet up on the sofa and drifted off to sleep.

He was awakened by the return of the colonel's wife laden with parcels from the shops. She set about preparing lunch. He rambled into the kitchen and sat down at the table, idly watching her as she busied herself on preparations for the meal. He put her in her late thirties, there must be up to twenty years between herself and her husband, he decided. She was light on her feet and had an athlete's poise. A saddle was sitting across the back of one of the chairs and a bridle hung from a hook behind the closed outside door.

His eyes strayed to her bruised face again and although she had her back to him she was sensitive to his gaze, and he saw her neck redden slightly in embarrassment.

Muldowney took his eyes away and asked her about her horses. She was suddenly brighter, more enthusiastic about her day. Horses, Muldowney decided, were very much part of her life. The grey in the field had been a gift from a friend who had gone away, and the pony had been bought for the boy although he was still too young to do much more than ride out beside her on a leading rein. There were other horses in fields around the back, she told him, and when she had put pots on to steam, she brought him outside to see them.

It as well after mid-day now and the winter sun was warm in the sky. The early rain had stopped for a while, and although the grass and the hedges were wet it was a kind and pleasant morning, one which fitted in extremely well with Muldowney's mood.

"Have you lived here long," he enquired.

It was her own family's house, she told him. She had inherited it when her father died, and when her husband had worked his way past the lower officer ranks and gained staff officer status they had been able to give up their rented house near the Curragh and settle in her old home. Muldowney had struck up a rapport with the woman in the few brief hours that he had known her. He liked the boy as well, and he had thrust the reason for his visit to the back of his mind. It stayed there until the army car turned into the drive and the colonel intruded once again.

He was surprised to see Muldowney, and although there was a flicker of alarm in his face when he first encountered the visitor in his house, the soldier was much more confident than during their first meetings. Now that the danger of prosecution and exposure from the brothel raid had apparently passed he was resentful of the treatment he had received from Muldowney and his team. His face was well flushed and although he was only marginally unsteady on his feet, Muldowney knew that he had a good deal of drink taken.

Muldowney's liking for the soldier's wife only heightened his contempt for the man himself. He had sympathized with O'Connor in his predicament but now having met his wife he could only dislike him. How could a man go off and look for hired women while he had a wife like this at home.

The soldier caught something of Muldowney's dislike and became more aggressive.   He began to bluster demanding to know what the agent was doing in his home and told him to leave. His wife hearing the altercation came into the room and he ordered her roughly back into the kitchen. Muldowney cut him down to size almost instantly when he told him of the events of the previous evening and his surveillance of the visit to the German embassy. He left out that it was an accidental encounter, implying that the officer had been trailed all along.

Chastened once again, and now much more like the dispirited man who had been arrested at Mrs Conroy's dubious lodging house, O'Connor volunteered such information as he had. He evidently knew nothing of Muldowney's own straightened circumstances or about the finding of the body of the unknown man. All he had to tell was that he had been sent to the embassy to collect a package which he surmised contained either documents or money. He had to deliver it to the left luggage office in one of the city railway stations. He was told to post the receipt to a private address and he had done so. Muldowney believed him. It rang true, and just as on the escort mission, the officer had only been told enough to allow him to complete the job. This time Muldowney was certain that the soldier was holding nothing back.

"I don't understand why you people are so interested," he said. "This is an official mission cleared by the government."

His comment was completely at variance with the misgivings which had led him to break down during his first interrogation. He had known there was something wrong then, and he knew it only too well now.

"Cleared by someone in the government," Muldowney corrected. "We want to know who."

The soldier walked across the room to the sideboard and poured himself a drink.

"I don't believe this is happening to me," he burst out desperately.

Muldowney aimed a low verbal blow.

"If you hadn't been out looking for whores in a drunken state you wouldn't be in this mess," he said, overlooking the fact that he too had been caught up in similarly desperate personal difficulties by the colonel's aberrations.

He decided to give his condemnation an extra more vicious pungency.

"You fouled up your mission by getting caught in a brothel. It's as simple as that. You have only yourself to blame. I don't know how you could got off with a family like this at home."

It was the complacent voice of self satisfied Irish puritanism speaking. Muldowney was unmarried and had few women friends. Only once in fact had he had an intimate relationship with a woman and this had lasted no more than a few guilt ridden weeks.

The soldier got to his feet and threw his glass into the fireplace. He was angry now. The sudden flying uncontrollable rage induced by continuous alcohol intake. Muldowney could see the anger physically convulsing him. His wife came into the room drawn by the smashing glass and raised voices.

She knelt down at the fireplace to pick up the broken pieces and the soldier pushed her away. Half kneeling she was caught off balance and fell over. O'Connor aimed a kick at her prostrate figure and Muldowney jumped forward in an attempt to intervene. The soldier swung at him, tripped over a chair and fell. The woman scrambled to her feet and retreated into one corner. The soldier despite his years and drunken state was on his feet again within moments and heading for Muldowney with arms flailing.

Muldowney lifted a small table, side stepped and hit him over the head. The table disintegrated , the soldier grunted in a heavy rush of expelled breath and fell forward on the hearthrug. Muldowney dragged him into a chair and tied his hands behind him with a flex from a lamp. After a few moments he came around and glared balefully at his captor.

The secret agent went to the fireplace and picked up a poker. He waved it angrily in the soldier's face. O'Connor drew his head as far away as he was able, his rage now turned to fear. Once again he was the stricken heap of a man that Muldowney had encountered after his arrest. The agent looked at him contemptuously. It didn't take much to put him down. He hoped that this wasn't the calibre of the rest of the Irish army.

"I want the full truth," the secret agent demanded fiercely.

He kept up the pressure for a few more minutes, but the soldier could tell him nothing more. Muldowney sat down in a chair opposite and stared at his prisoner.

He was certain that the soldier was telling the truth. He was only a go between, a weak man being used by others to carry out an important but nonetheless fairly mundane role. He had been carrying out orders, albeit illicit ones, but nothing more.

The sound of hooves on the gravel outside distracted him and he went to the window. The woman was riding out on her grey horse, obviously deciding to get away at least for a while from the turmoil of her home.

It was a turmoil, Muldowney suspected, that was very often present. He watched her as she walked the horse to the gate and listened to the diminishing pound of the horse's feet as she trotted off up the road. It was obviously not the first time that she had ridden off to escape the unhappiness of her married life.

Muldowney considered his next move. He was undecided. He knew he had to leave the soldier's house and carry on with his investigations. His own safety depended on a favourable outcome and it could not be too long delayed. At the same time he didn't want to leave the soldier free to raise the alarm. He thought things over for a moment, then dragged the officer, still tied to the chair, into the hall. There was a walk in cupboard under the stairs and he pulled the prisoner into it, tired his legs to the front legs of the chair and stuffed his handkerchief into the officer's mouth as a gag.

"You can stay in here until your wife comes back," he said. "She'll let you loose then."

He closed the door and turning the key went down the corridor to the kitchen. There was no sign of the boy. He called him once or twice without response and decided that he had taken himself off on some errand of his own. It was just as well, Muldowney decided. At least he had been spared the trauma of the struggle, although the sight of his mother getting a belt across the face as probably nothing new to him.

Muldowney caught a bus back to the city. He got off at Donnybrook and walked the half mile or so down Shrewsbury road to the German embassy. The tall German diplomat was now the only link he had with the bullion. O'Connor was a dead end, he was sure of that. There was nothing further to be got from him. His final offering had been the address to which he had posted the left luggage ticket. But the post would not arrive there until the following morning, a good eighteen hours away. In the meantime, he could not afford to waste any opportunities.

He rang the embassy bell with very little idea of how he was going to proceed. It was answered by a small slight man in a dark tightly fitting waistcoat. Muldowney described the official he had come to see, stumblingly offering as an excuse the fact that he couldn't remember the foreign name. The butler came smartly to his rescue. He had come to see the commercial attaché, the butler informed him. He was Herr Arnhold Mannheim. Muldowney was slightly surprised. He had expected to hear a more impressive name with a military rank. A mere commercial attaché did not at first impression appear to be the kind of diplomatic level that involvement in a plot to divest the Irish state of a large amount of its gold reserves would entail.

Muldowney gave his name, said that he had come on official business and waited until the butler returned. He was brought upstairs and into a surprisingly small room where the unobtrusively named Herr Mannheim sat behind a small desk.

Muldowney produced his card and showed it to the attaché. It did not strike any apparent degree of terror into the German official who invited him to sit down in the single chair that was available to visitors. Evidently not too many people came to beard Herr Mannheim in his den. Muldowney was suddenly at a loss. How was he to explain his visit, and what authority did he have over this official of a foreign state who would undoubtedly claim diplomatic immunity, and perhaps refuse to answer any questions if the Irish agent pushed him too hard.

To the secret agent's surprise the German took neither course. He answered each of Muldowney's questions with practiced openness, adopting an air of apparent puzzlement at their nature and the querying of his connection with the Irish army officer.

There was apparently nothing to hide. O'Connor had collected documents relating to a shipment of gold which the embassy had processed. There was nothing underhand about the arrangements. The gold was being flown from London to Frankfurt at the request of the Irish government. After that, its destination apparently was Switzerland. Mannheim repeated his assertion that the only role that the embassy had in the matter was one of facilitating movement of the bullion at the request of the Irish authorities.

The German's claim that the gold had been sent to Germany at the request of the Irish government confused Muldowney even further. The banker Rodgers had been quite definite that the gold was bound for the Bank of England. This was a whole new dimension.

Muldowney looked squarely into the bland suave face of the German diplomat. Although he was calling himself Herr Mannheim, the Irish agent had no doubt that he was sitting across the desk from a former officer who had served his country in the army of the Third Reich. He judged the German to be in his late fifties. He was polished, spoke English well, and made no effort at evasion or concealment in his responses. Their conversation was the easy casual exchange of questions and answers between one official and another. They could just as easily have been discussing the exchange of fruit and vegetables as bullion. Muldowney pressed him again about the change of destination without result. The attaché had done exactly as he had been requested by the Irish authorities and arranged diplomatic clearance out of Germany.

Every response the German made was easy, unhurried, delivered slowly due to the diplomat's apparent search for words in English, but every phrase evincing a straightforward uncomplicated reply. It looked good and it sounded good, but Muldowney's nose told him that underneath the urbanity, the veneer, lay a skilful camouflaging of the truth. Formally announcing himself satisfied, Muldowney rose to leave. The German escorted him downstairs and stood in the doorway just as he had done the previous evening when O'Connor had left the embassy. It was apparently his normal method of seing off his visitors.

Muldowney walked slowly back from the pleasant tree lined affluent suburb to the more proletarian center of the city. He stepped into a shop doorway when he caught sight of a police car coming towards him, but it went on and he resumed his walk. His mind ranged feverishly over the events of the day. The only other item of note that he had produced was the address to which O'Connor had posted the luggage ticket. Apart from that the Irish soldier and the German diplomat seemed to be played out as far as any further unraveling of the mystery was concerned.

Once again his mind returned to the unspoken question which lurked behind the entire sequence of events. What if his suspicions were nothing more than a series of conjectures which would be proved to be without foundation, hyped up into reality by the agent's own fevered desire to produce something worthwhile to save his career and in turn seized upon by the spymaster Queally to protect his department. The German's disclosure that the Irish officials had authorized the change in route seemed to support this possibility.

As matters stood the three people that he had met who were directly linked with the shipment of the bullion, O'Connor, Rodgers and the German official, the last two could in fact be totally innocent parties. There were, however, very positive additional factors which made Muldowney sure that he wasn't following any will of the whisp imaginary trail with his pursuit of O'Connor.

One was the fact that he himself was being hunted in connection with the finding o a murdered man where Cronin had dumped the brass bars, and the second was the fact that O'Connor on his own admission had brought the shipping documents to the left luggage office and posted off the reclaim ticket. Such a method of transmitting vital documents was not carried out in innocence. The bullion had disappeared. That was also a fact. But had it been taken by low life criminals or important people in the administration?

He went to a telephone kiosk and phoned Queally in his office. The spymaster listened intently to his subordinate's report. Muldowney, he decided, had two options. He could intercept the soldier's letter when it arrived at its destination in the morning post, or he could follow the recipient to the station and allow him to collect the holdall.

Queally turned it over several times while his agent waited at the other end of the telephone. To wait until morning would risk whoever was in the house getting away. He made up his mind.

"We'll meet you outside that address," he told Muldowney. "I'll bring Cronin. We'll raid it now and arrest the occupants."

Muldowney said he would be there and hung up. He caught another bus and got off in Rathgar, another suburb of genteel anglicized squares and bowling greens, not perhaps as overtly rich as the embassy territory of Ballsbridge, but nonetheless a comfortable oasis of prosperous Dublin life well removed from the small north city artisans' cottages and tenements with which Muldowney was more familiar.

He almost walked right into Queally's trap, but a secret agent's ingrained sense of self preservation was rapidly developing as one of the most powerful of the beleaguered operative's repertoire of skills. This cautionary instinct made him stay hidden when he reached his destination and he was well concealed in a laneway when half a dozen police cars arrived. Some of the officers were in uniform, others, the Special Branch or G men as they were still often called by their detractors, were in civilian clothes.

Curiously enough none of them tried to enter the house which Muldowney had identified as the destination of the letter. They stationed themselves around the area, parking their cars in alleyways. That meant only one thing. They weren't there to arrest the occupants. They were there to capture the secret agent.

Muldowney cursed Queally for a double dealer and dispelling the momentary fear that had gripped him when the squad cars arrived, allowed himself a congratulatory surge of satisfaction. He was learning the game too well. He had deliberately given the spymaster the wrong address. The real location was a different square. Had the police in fact been sent to raid the house that they were presently outside, the innocent occupants would have been in for an unpleasant surprise. There would have been angry and apologetic senior officers calling for Queally's blood within a few hours. It was clear, however, that there was going to be no such raid on the house. The police were there solely to capture the secret agent. Queally could then deal with the recipient of the letter at his leisure.

Muldowney watched for a few moments as the police took up positions which would allow them to intercept the unwitting secret agent had he been foolish enough to fall into their trap. Then he fled silently down the lane and made his way well out of the area, sticking to the endless maze of lanes and sidestreets that at the turn of the century and before had provided the servants, grooms and coachmen of the way with access to the stables and servant's entrances of the houses in which they laboured. Once again the spymaster had sold him out. Once again he was one the run. Once again he was alone.

He was desperate, but not as forlorn as he had been when his mission had first started to go wrong. He was still one step ahead of the spymaster. He knew the real address to which the letter had been posted. If he could get the ticket and then the holdall containing the documents, he would have a strong hand which even Queally would find difficult to countermand. In the meantime he had to get through another night without any place to stay.

Chapter Nine

Muldowney spent the night in someone's garden shed and in the morning made his way to the house where the letter was to be delivered. He went to the rere and easily forced a wooden gate that was set into the garden wall. The garden was well cared for. There were shrubs and winter plants, the grass kept short by the lack of growth in wintertime.

He had still at least two hours to wait, but he had to get himself in place to capture the letter when it arrived. He got into the house itself as easily as he had entered the garden gate. He was in a cellar below the kitchen, a room which itself perhaps had once been a downstairs kitchen, although it was now disused. Making sure that the communicating door to the rest of the house could be opened, he settled down to wait.

There was no sound from overhead, and the occupants whoever they were, were evidently accustomed to sleeping late. Muldowney took out the piece of paper on which he had scribbled the address. The name was innocuous enough, but curiously it was to a woman, Mrs Joyce Dolan.

He sat back on an old sofa and closed his eyes, thinking over his strategy. A great deal would depend on whether the postman came to the square early or late. If he came early enough there was a chance that the occupants of the house, whoever they were, would still be in bed. If he came late, then things would be much more difficult.

The agent ran a hand over his chin. He was dirty after his night in the shed, and even though he had been able to wash up at the officer's house, he hadn't shaved for forty eight hours. Muldowney realized that he cut a squalid figure, hopefully he would appear to be a desperate one too if there was any question of having to seize the letter by force. He wondered what Queally was going now, and let his lip curl in amusement at the spymaster's predicament. Queally, he felt sure, would have slept as uneasily as himself, although the spymaster would have been in more comfortable surroundings and would at least have had food.

He tried to put himself in Queally's place. The Director would by now have realized that he had been outsmarted. He would blame the police for not having captured the secret agent the previous night, and conceal the fact that Muldowney was more than just a man on the run. It would be too devastating an admission to have to disclose that he had vital information as well.

There was some movement upstairs and the pipes in the house groaned. Muldowney went up a short flight of stone steps and cautiously opened the communicating door. It led into the hall. He swore inwardly when he saw that there were no carpets, only highly polished wooden flooring with a couple of rugs thrown over it. A grandfather clock ticked at one end. A hallstand with some hanging coats, and sticks and umbrellas in the holders, stood between him and the front door with its overhead halfmoon leaded window. There was a telephone on a small table. The early sun was streaming through the window panes. There were several doors leading to dining room, lounge and kitchen, Muldowney decided. An elegantly railed staircase led upstairs.

The sound of feet on the landing drove Muldowney back into the cellar again. Someone came downstairs and went into the kitchen. He could hear the sound of a kettle being filled and a few items being put on a table. A chair scraped on a flagged floor and the breakfast maker sat down to start off the day. It was a short enough repast, evidently nothing more than tea and toast, Muldowney decided. The footsteps came into the hall again, paused for a few moments then walked to the front door. Seconds later it banged shut behind whoever had left the house.

Muldowney took off his shoes and padded silently to the front door, peering out through one of the tall narrow sidewindows. A smartly dressed middle aged woman was going out through the gate, a handbag on her arm, evidently on her way to work. The house was silent. Instinctively Muldowney knew that it was empty. He went swiftly and silently upstairs, checked each room and satisfied himself thatthere was no one there..

He paused for a few moments in one of the large front bedrooms. It was the one which had been occupied. The bed clothes had been thrown back and there was a faint scent of powder and perfume. He took a quick look inside a heavy ornate wardrobe, saw that it was well filled with smart expensive looking clothes and turned his attention to a three mirrored matching dressing table. It was littered with make-up bottles, perfumes, and silver backed hairbrushes and matching handmirror, and all the items which a sophisticated woman needed to utilize before she presented herself to the world.

The sound of mail dropping through the letterbox summoned Muldowney downstairs again. Half a dozen letters were lying on the floor. He scooped them up and retreated to the kitchen. Two of them were bills, one or two obviously letters from friends, one from England and the other from France. It was not too difficult to pick out the one he wanted, written in a scrawled, hurried hand and posted in Dublin the previous day. He tore it open and allowed his pent up breath to escape. The numbered ticket lay on the table in front of him.

He made himself some breakfast and then went upstairs to the bathroom to wash. He found a man's safety razor and spare blades in a shaving cupboard and then realising that the water was hot decided to have a bath as well. He lay back in the warm soothing water and reviewed his situation.

Once again he tried to put himself in Queally's position. What would the spymaster do now. He thought it out carefully and came to the conclusion that his best and most likely response would be to mount surveillance at each of the city's main railway stations, Kingsbridge, Amiens street, and Westland Row. There were, of course, the two smaller suburb serving stations, Harcourt street and Tara street, but he thought that Queally would discount these. It was, he felt sure, the bigger stations that would come to mind. In fact O'Connor had left the holdall in Tara street, the little station beside the Liffey which served mainly to take passengers from the city centre to the tiny halts of the southern suburbs and the mailboat at Dun Laoghaire.

Muldowney wrapped a towel around himself and went into the woman's bedroom and lay down. The bed was still warm from its occupant of the previous night, but although drowsy he didn't go to sleep immediately. His mind was still actively seeking the way forward. He decided that there was no immediate hurry. He could let Queally and his men stake out the stations for as long as they liked, but they didn't know what sort of bag they were looking for, and Queally could not risk the exposure of his dilemma by seizing every bag lodged in each of the Dublin railway left luggage offices. No, Muldowney decided, Queally would stake out the three main stations waiting for the agent to arrive in person.

Muldowney saw that for the moment he had the advantage. He decided that he would lie up in the house for the day and make his way through the city again under cover of darkness. He could either collect the bag at the counter if Queally's men were not in place, or break in during the night.

Satisfied with his decision he allowed himself to drift off into an exhausted sleep. He had not grasped just how much he had put himself through over the previous few days, and he was still asleep when the woman returned. The realization that someone had come into the room brought him out of his stupor and he awoke to find the woman standing over him. He

119

pulled the bedclothes up around him and sat up.

She was unalarmed, an amused smile playing round her lips.

"Well, well," she said, once she saw that he was awake. "Look who's sleeping in my bed."

Muldowney ignored the flippancy of the reference to the childhood fairy tale and cast desperately around the room in search of succour. His clothes were still in the bathroom. She laughed out loud and obviously totally unafraid went to the small armchair and sat down. She was in her early forties, Muldowney decided, a good looking, sophisticated Dublin woman, obviously accustomed to the good things of life. The style and furnishing of her house had already testified to that, but now that the secret agent could see the owner in person, he could see that the house and householder were well matched.

"What are you doing in my house," she asked. "To say nothing of my bedroom."

Muldowney was caught short for an explanation.

"I'm sorry," he said lamely. "I was waiting for you to come home."

Embarrassed by the fact that he was naked under the bedclothes he gestured helplessly with one hand.

"I was tired. I've been short of sleep for the past few days."

The woman took a packet of cigarettes from the dressing table beside her and lit up. She offered the packet to Muldowney who refused. He didn't smoke, although there was no doubt that a lighter and cigarette would enhance the appearance and effect of a secret agent in many circumstances.   Muldowney had seen a fair few Bogart pictures and had often envied the imagery which the gravel voiced tough talking screen bad man displayed.

"I'm Joyce Dolan," the woman introduced herself. "Who are you."

Muldowney told her his name and as quickly as his wits would allow came up with an excuse about coming to the wrong house by mistake. He didn't know whether she believed him or not but the explanation such as it was got over the immediate conversational difficulty of his presence.

"I left my clothes in the bathroom," he said. She got up and went down to the first landing bringing his clothes back in a bundle. She dropped them distastefully on top of the bed.

"They look as if they could do with a bath as well," she commented. "What have you been doing"

He told her the same story that he had used to the soldier's wife.

"I've been traveling," he said. "From England on the boat. I got a bit messed up coming in through the back."

His explanation of how he had got into the house evidently pre-empted her next question for she was silent for a moment.

She looked at him for a few seconds more and then got to her feet.

"You'd better get dressed," she said. "I'll be downstairs."

He put his clothes on as quickly as possible and followed her down. She was in the kitchen doing something at the cooker.

The unopened letters and the station ticket still lay on the table. Muldowney quickly crossed the room and picked up the ticket thrusting it into his inside pocket.

She laughed and he realised that she had known all along just what he was after. A new respect for this woman's ability to master a situation and even tease it along a bit grew on Muldowney.

"You didn't have to break into my house to get that," she said. "I know it is important but you could have collected it by knocking on the door."

Muldowney said nothing. He sat down at the table and ate the short fry that she set down in front of him. He couldn't understand why she was so calm, so apparently fully at ease.

"I thought Malachy would come for it himself," she said. "But I suppose he has been busy. I knew it would be in the post, but I didn't think it was so urgent that you would come like this."

Muldowney finally got a grip on the situation. She thought he was a legitimate messenger for the ticket. That was why she was so unconcerned. But that meant also that someone could come to claim it at anytime. The busy Malachy himself for instance or a messenger.

"Malachy might come himself," he improvised. "I'll wait for a bit and see. It will save me a delivery later on."

The woman nodded.

"That's fine. I haven't seen him for a day or two. He's been away. Some government business, but I'm expecting him."

Muldowney sharpened up at this. Government business.

Perhaps now he was on to a real lead. The absent Malachy, whoever he was, had to be a very strong player, perhaps even the top man in the affair.

Joyce brushed past him to get something from a dresser and put her hand on his shoulder for a moment. He smelled her perfume and momentarily sensed that a slight bond of intimacy had been established. She was much older than the women he had been used to, clerks in the postal Department, nurses, shop girls from the stores around town, typists from the multitude of city offices.

Muldowney had little real experience of women. His occasional relationships with girls had been short lived, and he found himself somewhat in awe of this obviously experienced and sophisticated woman. He had liked O'Connor's wife as well. But she was a worn, ordinary, disappointed woman. Joyce Dolan was glamorous, dominant, exotic, certain and satisfied with what life had brought her.

She evidently lived alone, but judging by the razor in the bathroom was not totally devoid of male companionship. Where was her husband, he wondered. Was he the Malachy she had mentioned. Perhaps her husband had gone, and Malachy was a friend, or perhaps even a brother, coming to stay now and then.

She sat down opposite him at the table and lit another cigarette. She had a cup of tea in front of her and took a few sips. Muldowney felt her scrutiny and was ill at ease. Instinctively he knew that she was coming on a bit at him. Perhaps the sight of his shirtless shoulders in her bed had stirred her up a bit he reflected. He wondered what he should do. This was the third time in as many days that he had felt attracted to a women, first Veronica, then the soldier's abused wife, and now this very different, almost overpowering woman.

123

"Tell me more about yourself," she invited. "Do you work for Malachy."

Muldowney gave some half convincing answer, mumbling something about different duties, and steered the conversation around to the woman herself. She worked part time at the National Gallery, she told him, cataloguing exhibits which were in store for the nation but which the nation would never see given that funds for exhibiting were paltry.

"Malachy encouraged me to take up the job after my husband died," she observed. "He believes in the arts. If he weren't so busy he would do a lot more for cultural affairs."

"Is your husband long dead," he asked, deciding to rationalize her relationship with the absent Malachy as quickly as possible.

"He died about five years ago," she answered. "In St Luke's."

Muldowney nodded. He knew that she was explaining the unmentionable by naming the Dublin cancer hospital. She tapped her cigarette ash into her saucer.

"I suppose I'm asking for it as well."

Muldowney made an evasionary shrug and ploughed on in an effort to establish the identity of the elusive Malachy. Who was he and why had O'Connor sent him the left luggage ticket for the bullion consignment documents by such a roundabout route. The woman was an innocent party to the affair, he decided. But her Malachy was a different item altogether. More and more Muldowney was convinced that he was on the right track. There was no doubt in his mind now that he had stumbled across an attempt by someone high up in the government to steal the country's bullion from under the noses of its guardians.

THE IRISH SECET AGENT

The telephone rang and she went into the hall to answer it.

"That was Malachy," she said when she came back.

There was a tension in her now that had not been there before. Obviously Malachy had told her that her visitor was out of place.

"You're to wait," she said. "If you like."

She sat down again but was now openly ill at ease. Muldowney had no intention of going. He made an effort to relieve her anxiety.

"There's no need for you to worry," he assured her. "I'm sure there is an explanation."

She looked at him in surprise for a moment as if not fully understanding what he was saying, stubbed out her cigarette and stood.

"We'll be more comfortable in the lounge," she said.

He followed her to the front of the house.

Within twenty minutes a car drew up outside. It was a black state limousine with a plain clothes officer at the wheel. Muldowney got up and went to the window as the new arrival walked towards the house. He recognized him.

Finance Minister Malachy Finucane was not exactly an unknown personality. An astute politician, a lawyer by profession, he had achieved ministerial office within a year or two of is election to the Dail. The woman went to open the door and the secret agent recrossed the room and stood in front of the fireplace. The minister, a medium sized, smart looking man with a strong determined face, walked purposefully into the room. They stared at each other for a moment or two.

"Who are you," the politician asked finally.

Muldowney brought out his card. The minister fingered it for a moment and handed it back.

Facially he had given no indication of concern as he read the secret agent's identification but there was a slightly more tense edge to his voice when he spoke again.

"What are you doing here"

Muldowney brought out the luggage ticket.

"I'm here about the gold."

The minister looked at the ticket for a moment, partly stretched out a hand to take it but dropped his arm again as Muldowney moved away. The agent put the vital piece of paper back in his pocket.

The politician licked his lips. They were thin, almost bloodless lips, Muldowney saw, and the eyes were hooded over a haggard face. He realised that the politician compensated with power what he might lack in size and good looks.

"I'm investigating the situation," Muldowney said eventually.

The minister frowned.

"What are you, Special Branch."

Muldowney shook his head. He named his secret department and its reclusive head. The minister was perplexed. The arrival of Queally's man at this quiet suburban house was evidently an unexpected factor.

126

THE IRISH SECRET AGENT

Muldowney was at a loss as to how to proceed. He had located his quarry, as he thought, but he had run up against the power of superior authority. The minister was obviously not a man to submit to any pressure from a junior civil servant, secret agent or not. And there was still that niggling doubt in his mind. Was it possible that the involvement of anyone at this level after all a figment of his imagination. Had he just been confused by coincidence and peculiar circumstances.

At the same time he could see that the minister was worried. There was a tightness to his mouth, a calculating narrowness to his eyes, and his nostrils stiffened as he too considered the implications of this visit from an obscure but apparently authoritative agency which could stimulate and direct unwanted enquiries.

Finucane too was studying his adversary. The years of political deal cutting and sizing upu opponents had given him a fairly accurate measure of the secret agent's strengths. Here was a man doing his job but obviously out of his depth. The agent was a man who was a long way down the ladder and could be controlled with fairly minimal effort. Finucane knew only too well that ambitious men in lowly roles could surrender all scruples when swayed by men who could further their careers.

He was only partly correct in this assessment. Muldowney had matured in several ways over the past few days. The euphoria of his bullion scoop had been succeeded by the pressures of his predicament and the realization that his own head of Section was playing a double game with him, promising back up and exposing him to the police at the same time. He was wary now, conscious that he was dealing with an important figure in the political hierarchy, perhaps even a confidant of the band of Grim Grey Men who wielded absolute power. At the same time he was determined that no matter how important an adversary the politician might be, he was not going to be hoodwinked as easily as before.

The politician made his move.

"The first thing we must do is collect these documents," he said. "After that we must get in touch with your superior and straighten out this matter."

Muldowney thought for a moment.

"Do you intend to collect the papers personally," he asked.

The minister shook his head.

"No, Joyce is going to do that. It's better that way."

Muldowney said nothing. He decided not to ask why documents relating to a genuine shipment should have to be moved around in such a fashion.

"I would be recognized," the minister said simply. "The success of this operation rests on it being carried out in secret. The country would be put at serious international commercial disadvantage if it were know that we had to prop up our currency with a draw down of our reserves."

For a moment Muldowney was mildly startled. It was the first time that there had been any semblance of an explanation of why the shipment could be a legitimate exercise.

There was another short silence and the minister spoke again.

"I suggest you stay here for the moment. Joyce can go down to the railway station with you later on. I have a number of meetings and functions this evening and I shall be tied up."

Muldowney thought it over.

"I will go as far as the station with Mrs Dolan," he said eventually. "That way I can be sure that there are no complications. We can arrange to meet at your office after that."

Finucane considered for a moment and agreed. He went to the hall and the woman followed. They spoke together quietly for a few minutes. The front door banged and the woman came back into the room.

She went to a drinks cabinet and brought out two sherry glasses and a bottle of Bristol Cream. Muldowney sipped thoughtfully and looked across the room to the woman seated in the armchair opposite.

"I'll make some dinner later on," she said. "After that we must wait for instructions. Malachy will ring and arrange a time to meet us."

Despite his suspicion Muldowney relaxed, the sherry and the broken sleep of the past several days making him drowsy. He could have done with another few hours in bed, he reflected. Joyce interrupted his thoughts by starting to make more conversation. Muldowney responded absently at first, then becoming more animated as they warmed to each other. He realized that she was drawing him out but saw no reason why he should be totally secretive about his background. He gave her a brief resume of his so far brief career in Queally's secret service.

He deliberately stayed away from discussing the current investigation and she didn't press him. He gave her a slightly more enhanced view of his status than was strictly true, and coloured in a few imaginary investigative adventures.

She was a good conversationalist and when she had obviously extracted all the information she was likely to get,   turned the conversation to other topics. Paintings and music seemed to be her main interests. Muldowney had little to contribute. His musical interludes were limited to occasional outings to the dances in the ballroom at the back of the Swiss restaurant in Merrion Row or to the Friday night jazz sessions at the Green Studio near the Russell Hotel on St Stephen's Green.

He asked her about her work in the National Gallery and listened sympathetically when she complained about the shortage of cultural funds that prevented the expansion of Ireland's world of art. She complained too that Dublin lagged behind other capitals in that there was no national concert hall. And this in a city where Handel had performed his Messiah. Muldowney felt the need to make some small gesture in defence of his country's cultural heritage, although his knowledge was scant enough.

"We have the Abbey," he remarked. "It is known all over the world"

"And now the plays are put on in the Queens," she rejoined sharply, referring to the fact that the Abbey Players were performing in the Pearse street theatre and that their burnt out home had still not been rebuilt.

"They're going to start a whole new building on the old site shortly," she went on.

Muldowney knew that as well. It had been in the papers lately.

"They've been talking about a concert hall as well for years," he said. This aspiration too had been in the papers.

She agreed.

"That will come in time as well."

She got up and walked to the window. Muldowney's eyes followed her in admiration. However, he felt that she needed to be answered. She was too convinced about the state's lack of investment in culture.

"Someday we'll have national television," he remarked sarcastically.

"Yes indeed," she replied composedly. "Malachy will see to that as well. It won't be too long now."

"It will be another ten years at least," Muldowney responded, this time with some authority.

The Section shared its headquarters with the national radio station and corridor gossip had given him some insight into the state of play of the drive towards television. It would come eventually, of course, but it would be driven more by the need to counter the aggressive inroads of immoral English channels and a narrowly focused desire to promote native Irish values on the small screen rather than a perceived need to provide more genuine entertainment.

She stood silently for a moment looking at the street outside. A poised elegant well dressed woman of the world was what Muldowney saw. Not for her the cheap shoes and dresses from Denis Guiney's emporium for the poorer middle classes. This was a lady who shopped in Grafton street, at Switzers and Brown Thomas, probably with a monthly charge account, he reflected.

Muldowney was very clear in his mind about the type of woman he admired. His career as a secret agent was hallmarked with fantasies about sophisticated glamorous female spies whom he felt sure must work in the wider espionage community overseas. He yearned for the days when he would be sent to work in the murky world of international espionage, perhaps recruited on secundment to the British secret service or to the CIA.

He had once written to Edgar Hoover and to the Russians via their London embassy offering them his services. Edgar Hoover had not replied. The Russians wrote back telling him that they didn't know what he meant by becoming one of their agents. He hadn't the courage to pursue the matter further.

Now, here, right in front of him was the real live woman of his dreams. Elegant, well coiffured, well dressed, living in a mini mansion in a part of the city to which he could not even aspire to rent a room, even if there was one available, in any of the surrounding gracious residences. His world was a far cry from this leafy suburb populated by families of Dublin people who had always been reasonably wealthy, whether under King and Castle, Free State, or the austere censored state of De Valera.

Muldowney felt almost limp with suppressed excitement. The entry of this latest woman, a really splendid femme fatale into the affair had really stirred his blood. This really was what life as a secret agent was all about. The hardships of the previous few days were put behind him, the fear and the uncertainty engendered by the calamities that had engulfed him were thrust aside. Suddenly reinvigorated, Muldowney felt that he could accomplish anything, take on any adversary, once he knew that this woman was at his side.

That he was suffering from a bout of spurious idealism and a half feverished imaginative view of life far divorced from reality did not occur to him at all. He had entered the half world of intrigue and money and power. It was a deeply satisfying state to be in.

The telephone rang again. She walked out to the hall to answer it, exchanged a few words and came back into the room.

"We have to go," she said. "It will take us at least an hour to get into town."

She looked at Muldowney with a degree of concern that was obviously more allied to his appearance than any degree of physical attraction.

"You need evening clothes," she said. "We have to go to meet Malachy at a reception in the Castle. We can't go there with you looking like that. Anyway you won't get in unless you at least have a dinner jacket."

She laughed at him without derision, but even so Muldowney was embarrassed. He looked down at his clothes. His trousers were stained and torn, his shoes unpolished and showing the signs of rough living, his light tweed jacket a comrade in dishevelment to its trouser companion. He followed her upstairs to one of the empty bedrooms and she brought out a dinner suit. It had been one of her late husband's, she told him.

"He was about your build," she commented.

A rummage in a chest of drawers secured a shirt, socks and underwear. She went out of the room while he quickly changed.

He looked at himself in the wardrobe mirror when he had dressed. It was remarkable what effect a good tailor could have one someone who had never in his life even been fitted for a suit. Muldowney, whose taste in clothes was dictated primarily by their price and the standard insignificance deliberately adopted by his fellow civil servants, saw himself a man transformed. He had never worn an evening suit before. No one in his family or circle of friends ever dressed for dinner or went to social functions which required formal attire. The black satin collared dress suit was an expensive version of

133

its kind and felt good to the touch. It fitted him surprisingly well. The shirt was lighter than his own and he didn't know how to tie the bow.

He padded downstairs in his socks to the kitchen and rummaged in one of the cupboards for polish and brushes for his scuffed, stained shoes.

"You can wear these."

She handed him a pair of men's patent evening shoes. They were a little tight but like the suit fitted well enough. She took the bow and deftly tied it. He could smell her perfume. She was wearing a fully shouldered medium length formal dress. A short white fur coat lay across one of the kitchen chairs.

She looked at him approvingly when he went back into the drawing room.

"You're a different person" she remarked. "You've cleaned up surprisingly well."

She was half joking, half in earnest, but Muldowney felt a degree of elation. Such praise from this woman was worth a week's pay. That her status in connection with his quarry was still undetermined, whether friend, associate, mistress, had yet to be discovered, did not deter him. Something new and exciting had come into his life and he was going to make the most of it.

They walked together towards the taxi rank. She moved him subtly, without any apparent criticism from her inside so that he walked between her and the street. It was a lesson in old fashioned etiquette that was not entirely lost on the secret agent. He reddened slightly and made an elaborate show of helping her into the flamboyant imported Studebaker. Irrationally Muldowney once again wondered as the taxi set off towards the city center why Dublin taxi divers preferred American cars when it must surely have been much cheaper to bring in standard black taxis from England. Perhaps it was the Dublin driver's way of showing that Ireland's capital was truly rid of England's crown, or perhaps there was an angle somewhere, and somebody had access to a profitable supply of transatlantic motors.

When they were set down in the centre of the city Muldowney decided it was time for him to take charge. As they walked towards the little station near the Liffey he gave his instructions in a low decisive voice.

"Go to the luggage office by yourself," he told her. "I'll keep you in view and make sure that we're not being watched."

She seemed surprised. He explained that there was a possibility that rival detectives might have the station under observation. She was silent for a moment or two as if taking on board the fact that there was an element of risk here that she had not understood before.

As it happened the exchange of the ticket for the holdall was accomplished without incident. Queally had not bothered with the suburban stations. If there were watching eyes they were focused on the three mainline stations that channeled travellers to the north, south, and west of the country. Muldowney had rightly surmised that Queally would not believe that the conspirators would risk such a small station for their dropping point. They left the station and simultaneously the minister's black state car with its police driver drew up beside them. The politician was in the back, like Muldowney wearing a dinner suit. Only the driver in his ordinary clothes now seemed out of place.

The minister opened the door for Joyce and told Muldowney to get in the front. Muldowney still had the holdall in his hand.

He settled himself in the front of the car and put it on his knees. Then making a sudden decision he pulled it open and took out the envelope. He could see the minister looking at him sardonically in the driver's mirror. In spite of this he opened the envelope and leafed through all the documents. There were up to a dozen sheets in all, quite obviously copies of invoices, delivery notes, manifests and transmission documents authorizing the transfer of the bullion from Dublin to London, to Frankfurt, and out of Germany to Switzerland.

There was one other item. It seemed to be a list of names, places, and dates. They were all foreign. He pored over it for several minutes but it meant nothing to him. Conceivably it could be a list of books and their authors. If so, the reader must have only been interested in history. Some of the dates stretched back for several hundred years. He gained nothing further from his scrutiny and folded everything back into its envelope.

The book list, if that indeed was what it was, was extraneous to the rest of the documentation. Although Muldowney knew that he had a complete paper trail in his hands which even gave the name of the destination bank in Switzerland, the secret agent felt a distinct sense of anti-climax. He had half hoped to find the holdall full of bank notes in large denominations. A payoff would be a more positive proof of skullduggery than a collection of duplicate delivery dockets and a possible list of historic books. The minister put out his hand and without further hesitation Muldowney obediently handed the envelope and its sheaf of papers into the back of the car.

Chapter Ten

The car picked up speed and traveled swiftly through the darkening city streets. They quickly passed Trinity College and headed up Dame Street towards Dublin Castle. Muldowney felt some slight pangs of alarm. Up to now he had some sort of edge from having possession of the luggage docket. Now he had handed over his small amount of insurance. Finucane could be driving him towards Queally and capture. However, he decided that for the moment he was safe enough. The minister would not want to risk any sort of incident in the presence of the police driver and the woman.

He looked at the silent detective at the wheel for a moment or two, wondering if he knew anything about the identity of his front seat passenger. He decided not. His changed appearance and the company of the minister must surely combine to ensure that he was most unlikely to be recognized from any description given to the police. Wherever they might be looking for the luckless secret agent, it was highly improbable that they would be searching for him at a state reception with a minister and his mistress.

The minister brought them up the wide staircase to the foyer of the reception area where the host of the evening, another more senior member of the cabinet was standing with his wife to welcome the guests to the reception. It was a gathering thrown for some visiting trade delegates, the state's official welcome to those who might at some stage bring some business to the hard pressed economy. De Valera's vision of families living happily on small holdings, growing their own foodstuffs and dancing at the cross roads was now well adrift in the ocean of reality, and the more perceptive members of his administration were casting their nets for more lucrative harvests.

They avoided the formal handshaking and few welcoming words in Irish from their host by following Malachy into a

137

connecting ante room which neatly sidestepped the handshaking hosts and allowed them to enter the reception chambers without hindrance. Finucane left his brief case in the cloakroom and brought them to a buffet where he handed them drinks and left, obviously intent on discussions with other government colleagues.

Muldowney was amazed at the gathering. He had never been at a state function before. Never even knew that such occasions occurred, and certainly never in his wildest imagination conceived that the small impoverished and struggling state could afford such a glittering event. The huge room was already crowded with people, all in formal evening wear, some indeed in tails. Bishops of both churches mingled with decorated glitterati from embassies and foreign communities resident in Dublin, captains of industry, and aging relics of revolutionary days. Their wives and daughters were there too, all gathered together to chatter, eat and drink where once they colonial administration had also thrown its hooleys.

His proximity to such importance and obvious wealth surprised the secret agent whose experience of life in the post war Irish state had been one of modest existence, steady employment for those who like himself were prepared to work for small return in the government service or for the equally sparse rewards of shop or occasional factory floor. The contrast could not in fact have been greater with the drab city outside the castle walls, where workless, haunted men paraded in search of jobs, and tinkers congregated round the city suburbs in dismal dirty camps.

There was a time, of course, when the Irish workers, reveling in their new found freedom from the Crown had suffered their unchanging deprivation in silence, but in recent times the streets had echoed with strident new calls for work from thousands of workless men who could not afford to take the boat in search of a better lifestyle. There was even an association of the unemployed and an English pacifist was protesting for rights for tinkers. It was becoming increasingly clear that meek acceptance of poverty was no longer an Irish option.

Muldowney stared almost transfixed at the men in the blue and green uniforms of the state, the bishops in Roman red and Anglican purple robes, and the ornate diplomats in formal fancy dress uniforms from a bygone era. The chattering pious matriarchs who hid behind the courtiers and the chieftains of De Valera's Ireland were making the most of their night out. They gulped their drinks as rapidly as possible and ate their way through mounds of ham, beef and chicken pieces, vegetable salads, rolls and deserts served by pressurised white clothed commis chefs and elderly sorefooted Dublin waitresses.

Of the ascetic emperor himself there was no sign. Dev did not like to be seen at such gatherings. Muldowney asked his companion about him.

"He doesn't come to these affairs," she replied. "Lemass is here though. That's him over there."

Muldowney caught a glimpse of the man who was starting to bring Ireland towards an industrialized economy. Stern, graying and determined, this was the leader who had been in waiting for many years, but who still walked in the shadow of the austere ruler who had governed them for a quarter of a century.

A sudden hush in the rising crescendo of voices turned their attention on the entrance. The crowd parted and Muldowney stared in astonishment. A tiny bald man accompanied by a large formidable woman stood there, apparently basking in the adulation which their appearance had created.   For a moment

Muldowney thought that his was the forerunner of some extraordinary cabaret act. The little man, red faced, rotund, was a cross between an extravagantly decorated large leprechaun and a garish Christmas tree. He was covered from almost head to toe in medals and ribbons with sashes slung across his front from both sides.

The crowd began to clap and the pair walked forward.

Joyce whispered in Muldowney's ear.

"That's Sean T. O'Kelly. He always comes to state parties."

Muldowney stared in even greater astonishment. Could it be that this vulgar grotesque apparition, clad in this most extraordinary collection of decorations covering every inch of his body and clinging even to the tails of his coat, was the nation's greatest living diplomat and former president.

"The woman with him is one of the Ryan sisters," Joyce explained.

The comment meant nothing to Muldowney. Two sisters or ten had no significance for him.

Muldowney couldn't take his eyes of the ornate apparition. It moved unsteadily forward, clinging to the strong arm of his tall companion, a few small steps at a time.

"He's well past it now, turning senile I should think judging by the get up they produce him in."

Joyce's contempt for the manner in which the little man was exhibited was apparent in her voice.

Muldowney said nothing. Certainly the tiny man in his ribbons and ornaments was the most outlandish parody of decorated

140

distinction that the had ever seen.

"What are all those things," he asked.

"He is the most decorated man in the country," she replied. "Most of the stuff is foreign."

The clapping died away and the incongruous couple made their way to chairs at the side of the room and sat down. The crowd moved forward and they were lost from view.

Muldowney got himself another gin and tonic and looked around at the rest of the gathering. It was now a flushed and merry party. The high hum of several hundred conversations reached to the ceiling again as the excitement of the diminutive senile statesman's arrival died away.

Finucane came back and ignoring the secret agent began to converse with Joyce. Muldowney slid quietly away. The drink was beginning to affect him, and he felt a little queasy. He took a jug of milk from the tea counter and swallowed several mouthfuls. No stranger to week-end drinking in the pubs at home, he had his own methods of resisting the power of intoxicants, although he seldom drank spirits. Kilkenny beer or the black pints from St James's Gate were his normal order.

He moved off by himself again and although no longer hungry took a piece of chicken from a platter and studied the scene once more. There must be four or five hundred people in the place, he decided. The contrasts in their appearance was quite startling. That there were many distinguished people in the room was true, but there were those whose clothes enhanced their appearance and those who were bursting out of badly fitting suits and were out of place despite the uniformity of evening dress and stiff white shirt fronts.

The men, he decided, were more generally presentable than

the women, many of whom were almost garishly dressed in ill fitting ostentatious clothes. There were others, however, who like the minister's mistress had obvious natural dress sense and the money to purchase Sybil Connolly style and elegance. The heady mixture of countless different brands of perfume and alcoholic fumes was stifling and Muldowney moved further away from the main crowd towards the less populated end of the room.

It was here that he encountered the German diplomat. Like Muldowney he was in an ordinary dinner suit, although the attaches from other embassies were in full dress uniform, but his reticence in apparel could not disguise his military background.

They shook hands in the formal Continental way and the German bowed slightly. He didn't click his heels though, a gesture which Muldowney had half expected. He didn't seem at all put out by Muldowney's presence and once again the secret agent marveled at the bland acceptance of the bullion movement as being a run of the mill innocuous transaction.

Muldowney racked his brains for some way of turning this unexpected meeting to his advantage, but there seemed little that he could say to elicit any further information. The diplomat had been totally forthcoming during their conversations at the embassy. At that moment, the minister turned and caught sight of both of them standing together. A quick frown crossed his face and he left his companion on her own and started across the room towards them.

Once again Muldowney could sense from the other's expression and body language that he was on the right track. The minister was concerned at this chance meeting. Muldowney stood his ground. Finucane reached them, affable enough, shook hands with the German and once again shouldered the agent aside.

Muldowney realized that he was up against a man who knew how to dominate. This was a man who wielded power, who knew how to control people and events, was accustomed to giving orders and having them carried out. He knew how to sideline people, destroy their careers, humiliate them, and could do so with total ruthlessness.

Once again Muldowney understood just how vulnerable he was. That Finucane was keeping him on a string for some reason was quite evident. Muldowney could, of course, go to Queally and directly implicate the minister but without the documentation he had no hard evidence. The whole saga in fact was hearsay. The only hard fact was that the bullion had not reached its destination, but Muldowney realized that even that particular event could be covered up. He needed some personal insurance. The money trail could only be followed through its various stages by the production of the sequence of authorization, the first and most damning document of which was the sheet which had been signed by the minister himself. The trail led back to Finucane, but he had covered his tracks by factoring a layered structure of assistants who knowingly or not had moved the operation a step forward and handed on to the next man.

A photographer was taking pictures around the room, the spasmodic burst of light from his flash gun bouncing off the chandeliers and the medals of the glittering assembly. Struck by an idea, Muldowney followed him around from group to group until he decided to take a break and the agent moved in on him. A few words, an agreement on a fee, and both went to the cloakroom. Muldowney lifted the minister's brief case from its cubby hole and took out the bundle of papers. Slowly, painstakingly, his companion photographed each sheet as Muldowney held it up in front of his chest. It seemed to take forever, the photographer labouring over the changing of each plate and packing it carefully into his carrying case.

Muldowney replaced the sheets as he had found them and returned the brief case to its place. He took a card from the photographer and made arrangements to collect the prints the following day. Then he went back to the reception where the minister and the German were deep in conversation.

Muldowney rejoined Joyce. She was still alone, a fact which the secret agent found a little strange, given her undoubted attractiveness. He grasped immediately, however, that there was a reason for this. It was the fact that she was the known confidante of a rising member of the government. Everyone who mattered probably knew of the liaison. If directly confronted by the two of them together, they would accept them, but there was no acceptance for such a woman on her own.

Mkuldowney felt a personal bond of sympathy for her loneliness, but if she was experiencing such a sensation she gave no sign. She welcomed him back with a smile and their conversation turned to more general things.

The agent kept a worried eye on the photographer. He was still taking groups of people around the room, but Muldowney knew that his stock of plates for the heavy graphic camera would soon run out, and hopefully he would leave.

There was, of course the possibility that he might remain and mingle, but Muldowney knew that the man would have been out on countless similar occasions, and would probably want to do nothing more than get home. And so indeed it proved. The man used what was evidently his last plate, put away his camera and headed for the door. Muldowney breathed a sign of relief. At least that episode had been successfully accomplished.

The minister came back to them.

THE IRISH SECRET AGENT

"I have to leave now," he said. "More state business."

He turned to Muldowney.

"I would like you to stay with Joyce tonight," he said. "You will oblige me by coming to my office in the morning. I'll send my car back to collect you in half an hour or so."

With that he was gone. Muldowney knew that he was still on a leash but was relieved too. There was no way he could have taken off into the dark clad in a dinner suit, and at least the Rathgar house would give him a bed and shelter for the night. There was another aspect of the arrangement which appealed to him. He was being given the opportunity of spending more time with Joyce Dolan.

The rest of the evening was uneventful. There was obviously no question of them embarking on a different kind of relationship. She made no overtures and driving home in he minister's car, he worked out his strategy for the following day.

He was awake well before dawn and quietly went through Joyce Dolan's late husband's wardrobe for a change of clothes. His own now were too disreputable to wear and would have attracted notice. Re-equipped, he stole quietly down to he bathroom, shaved and went downstairs. The woman's handbag was lying on the kitchen table and he rifled it without compunction. He took the few pounds that it contained and left the house.

He walked into the city which was slowly coming to life. The street lights were switched off and a murky grey day began to emerge. Within an hour he was outside the photographer's studio. The man let him in and brought him down a flight of stairs to his darkroom. The photographer slipped each developed plate into an enlarger and allowed the light to dwell on the sheet of photographic paper for a few seconds. Fascinated, the secret agent watched as the images slowly emerged in the developer. The photographer dropped each sheet into fixer, washed it off and then hung it up on a line to dry.

Muldowney counted out some of the notes he had taken from Joyce Dolan's handbag and held them out to the photographer. The man shook his head. He grinned conspiratorially at the secret agent.

"That's not half enough," he said. "I can see what these papers are about. Shipments of gold. You want my silence. I want my cut."

Muldowney threw the notes on the bench and moved towards the hanging prints. The photographer tried to stop him. Without thinking Muldowney shot out a fist and hit the man full in the face. It was a hard vicious effective blow. The man dropped instantly, hitting his head of the heavy stoneware sink as he went down.

Muldowney stepped across him and taking the prints off the line put them through the glazer to finish off. He found an envelope large enough to take the prints then turned his attention to the stricken man on the floor. He wasn't breathing. Blood was oozing from a wound to his head. Muldowney slapped is face once or twice, then hit him in the chest but to no avail. A cold desperation swamped him as he realized that the man was dead.

Muldowney left the building as soon as he was certain that there was nothing he could do for the stricken photographer. He walked hurriedly through the now much busier streets putting as much distance as he could between himself and the photographer's studio. He sat in a café and ordered tea and toast to fill the void in his stomach and desperately wondered what he should so. He had killed a man. Secret agents did it all the time. But this hadn't taken place in a dramatic shoot out with an armed opponent. It was a sordid accident in trivial circumstances. None the less he might have a hard job to prove himself innocent of any intent.

He tried to reassure himself that such happenings were part and parcel of the life of a secret agent, and that in any case he had come and gone undetected. No one would be able to link him up with the photographer. It was at that point that he realized that he had left a telling clue behind. There were six developed photographic plates lying beside the dead man's enlarger. Had he left fingerprints as well.

Muldowney sorted through the prints keeping them hidden under the café table in case he was overlooked. Then he put them back in the envelope and wondered what to do next. Now more than ever, he had to ensure that they were safe. But he was on a knife edge. On one hand he had evidence that outlined all the stages of a possible conspiracy. On the other hand he had left behind the sources of that evidence which could also prove that he had killed a man. Muldowney's head began to spin and he succumbed to a few moments of panic. Then he got back some self control. He fought to get his thinking in order.

The photographs had to be put in a safe place. He toyed with the idea of putting them back in a left luggage office. Then he decided that this time, Queally and indeed other agencies of the state would have no qualms about going through all the left luggage offices in the city if they got an inkling that there was anything to be found. He could post them to an accommodation address somewhere, but that too would only give temporary respite. He needed a long term place of safety.

He went out into the street again and walked towards College Green. He was careless. He might be recognised, but instinctively feeling that he was now well enough dressed not to attract attention and that few people would know him anyway. It would only be sheer bad luck that might bring him face to face with someone he knew and who also knew that he was on the run.

He turned into Dame street and was passing the imperious offices of one of several banks there when he was struck by an idea. Banks were safe, secure and confidential. He turned into the portalled entrance of the Royal bank and told a cashier that he wanted to open an account. He was asked to wait and after about ten minutes or so was shown into the manager's office.

Here was a man who enjoyed being a bank manager and although well past middle age was jolly, active, and as smartly suited as Muldowney himself. He added an air of cheerfulness to his formal business appearance by sporting a red rosebud in his buttonhole. Muldowney liked him immediately, although he could sense that behind this outward veneer of affability and good fellowship there lurked a keen and calculating brain.

Muldowney had briefly rehearsed his approach while he waited. He gave his name, his home address down the country and Social Welfare number and said he wanted to open a small savings account. He tendered a five pound note. The manager accepted it without demur. Small steady accounts from people in small steady jobs, saving for the future was just the kind of safe steady business that banks liked to encourage in their role of guardians of thrift and economy.

The bank manager accepted Muldowney at face value. His story had the ring of truth which indeed it nearly was, and Muldowney was confident that even if the bank had sought confirmation, his previous incumbency in the Department of Social Welfare would be still fresh enough in that department to have it upheld. Once a civil servant always a civil servant. Only a job with Guinness had a better recommendation for a working man in search of credit.

Muldowney put the precious envelope up on the desk.

"I would like to leave this for safe-keeping as well," he said. "It contains some family papers. I don't want to keep it around my flat."

The bank manager got up and found an envelope larger than Muldowney's own and slipped the smaller one inside. He wrote his new customer's name and his account number on the Outside and then brought out a stick of sealing wax from a drawer, put a match to one end and dropped a small blob onto the closed tongue of the envelope.

"Now," he said cheerfully. "This will be as safe here as if it were in the bank."

They both laughed at his little joke and after a few more moments of conversation, Muldowney picked up his deposit book and left.

He stood on the steps for a moment watching the roaring traffic as it headed for O'Connell bridge. He walked in the same direction and when he came to the Liffey, turned down along the quay for a few yards, and leaning over the stone parapet tore his newly acquired pass book into shreds and threw the pieces into the grim waters below. His secret hiding place was all the more secure if he kept its location in his head. After that he moved quickly back into the concealment of the crowd.

Chapter Eleven

Once again Queally sat across the Committee Room table from the Grim Grey Men. The spymaster was temporarily shorn of his veneer of obsequious certainty. The summons had come without any preliminary skirmishing. Queally was to appear immediately and bring his file on the bullion case with him. The terse command from a higher civil servant had begun and ended without any courtesies whatever.

He had gone to the government offices in Merrion Square as quickly as possible but was totally unprepared for the information he was to receive. The police Commissioner passed him in the corridor. They passed by without comment, indeed Queally only half noticed the state's highest ranking uniformed policeman. There was nothing unusual about his being in the building. The Security Committee was often brief on serious matters by the Commissioner in person.

It was not until he had automatically started to recite a report on the matter in hand and was sharply cut off, that Queally realized that there were very serious issues on hand. He had nothing new to offer the Security Committee beyond the involvement of the German embassy and the assurance that his best agent was on a paper trail which would eventually lead to the uncovering of the eventual destination of the bullion and the identity of whoever had consigned it there.

They were weren't interested in this information and Queally fell silent, a numb chill enveloping as he listened to what the most senior of the ministers had to say. The usual five had been augmented by one more. Queally was surprised. The Minister for Finance did not normally have a role to play in security.

"Your man has run amok," the committee chairman opened up on the spymaster with a belligerence that made Queally wince. "The Commissioner has brought us very disturbing information. There have now been three murders. Your agent has been linked to all of them."

He stared contemptuously at the spymaster, taking massive satisfaction from the very obvious fact that the news he had imparted was totally devastating to the man whose business it was to be the channel of such information. Now the positions had been reversed. It was the secret service chief who was being briefed with information that was definitely not to his satisfaction.

Queally cringed down in his seat. He had been hit hard. The Security Committee apparently had other sources of information. There were other agents at work, and what had started out as a minor intelligence triumph for his Section and under his control had exploded.

"Three murders," he repeated in stupefaction. "What ... I have no... Who has been murdered?

He eventually stuttered out the question that revealed he was totally out of his depth.

"You know nothing about them?'

The senior minister fixed the spymaster with an eye that reduced the normally controlled and self confident head of Section to pulp.

Queally shook his head. He could say nothing. His mouth was parched and dry and he knew that if he tried to speak all that he could produce would be a hoarse croak.

The Chairman picked up a sheet of paper.

"There have been three killings in three days," he said severely. "The unidentified man at the site of the material dumped by your officer, Cronin, and Colonel O'Connor who was found dead at his house last night. This morning a photographer was found dead in his studio. Your man Muldowney has been linked with each of these killings."

Queally stared at him in astonishment. He disregarded the case of the unknown man found with the brass ingots. That was old news. That O'Connor was dead was a total bombshell. He fought with himself for an appearance of control and asked about the soldier's death.

"We are surprised that you know nothing about this," the Chairman said. "You were supposed to have this man under close surveillance."

"Yes, yes," Queally stammered. "Muldowney..."

His words trailed off.

The minister nodded.

"Exactly," he said. "Muldowney. Your agent."

There was a long uncomfortable silence.

"What are the circumstances," Queally asked finally. He had not fully recovered his composure.

"Colonel O'Connor's body was found concealed in his house last night," the Chairman revealed. "He was tied up and hidden in a small room. However, it appears that the cause of death might actually be heart failure. We haven't had a post mortem result yet. Muldowney was identified as the man who tied him up. They had a fight in the house earlier yesterday."

There was silence again for a few moments. Queally said nothing. His mind was reeling with this extraordinary turn of events. He prided himself in his assessment of the men he hired. Muldowney was not a fighter. Exactly the opposite in fact. He had hired him because he was unassuming and unlikely even to be demanding or fixated on matters which affected him personally, never mind those which related to the job. For Muldowney to kill not one man, but three, was unthinkable.

"As for the photographer," the minister went on, "he was found a few hours ago. He died from a blow to the head. Muldowney has been connected to his death for the very good reason that he is in a number of photographs found at the scene."

The Chairman threw a batch of prints across the table. The police darkroom had concentrated on printing up Muldowney's face. The documents which he was holding in front of his chest and which should have been the primary field of the pictures were reduced and indecipherable.

Queally stared at them in silence.

"I don't understand," he said. "Why was Muldowney getting his picture taken?"

"Obviously for false identification papers," one of the other committee members cut in. He needed a false passport to get out of the country."

Queally's mystification was obvious but the spymaster's dilemma only served to heighten the exasperation of the ministers.

"This man has got to be caught," one of them remarked. "He has got to be put in jail."

The senior minister intervened.   He stared closely at Queally.

"Your department is not part of the ordinary policing and judicial structure," he said. "You report only to this Committee. You should be on top of events. We have a most serious situation here. An enormous amount of money belonging to the state has been stolen, obviously by this man Muldowney in collusion with others, and all witnesses are being systematically wiped out."

Queally started to protest. It just wasn't possible. The minister held up a restricting hand.

"Your agent was in league with O'Connor and the unknown man killed the night before. This is what we believe. They were all conspirators who either quarreled or are being eliminated as part of the overall conspiracy. We believe that the photographer was an innocent man to whom yhour agent went as a source of either prints or indeed complete passports. Muldowney killed him to silence him. He overlooked the plates in a rush to get away."

Queally again tried to remonstrate at these conclusions but he was waved to silence once more.

"The gold has gone to this man's head," the Chairman said sharply. He has become unhinged. As a matter of policy, to protect ourselves, we have told the police that he is to be hunted down. Every available resource will be put into this. But you are to get to him before the police."

Queally looked across at the senior minister. There was an obvious need for him to express a determination to get the job done.

"We'll find him," the spymaster responded as confidently as he could. "We'll find him," he repeated.

The Chairman spoke again. His tone was harsh and

uncompromising.

"You are to find him and kill him."

There was total silence in the room. Everyone there seemed to catch their breath as the enormity of what had just been said got through to everyone.

"Kill him," Queally repeated in astonishment.

The Minister spoke again.

"This man has made away with the country's gold and has killed three people in the furtherance of his operation. He is a madman. We believe that he has become deranged and he must be destroyed as quickly as possible.

The Justice minister intervened.

"Under no circumstances must any information about this missing bullion become public knowledge. Not even the police know that the shipment has been stolen. We intend to keep this a total secret. The commercial credibility of the country would be destroyed if anything leaked out. It would be better that we should lose the gold and have to replace it than have it searched for in a glare of publicity."

"Our country has many international financial enemies," the senior minister spoke again. "The international bankers and currency speculators have their own agenda. Nothing must be allowed to damage our interests."

Queally's head was spinning. Never before had he been given an instruction of this nature.

"Kill him. That would be murder," he said weakly. "How am I to do it. Where will I find him. Who is to kill him."

The Chairman looked over Queally's head at the wall behind him. It was decorated with a painting depicting some famous rebel encounter with the forces of the Crown in bygone eras of government brutality.

"This is an official order from the state," the Chairman said to him directly. There are numerous precedents."

Indeed there were, but there had been no clandestine executions for many years. The ministers knew that this was the first time that the current administration had made such an order.

That particular piece of information was not, however, to be imported to the squirming spymaster.

"You are the appropriate authority," the senior minister continued. "It is up to you to carry out the order. The duty of your department is to serve the government in every conceivable way. You are the hidden weapon of the Executive."

Queally latched on to the words order and authority.

"I shall need proper authorization," he said, tremulously clearing his throat.

The Chairman frowned.

"We have given you that authorization, here and now."

"I shall need it writing," Queally said. "For the record."

One of the grey men laughed. It was a grim, hard, mirthless sound.

"There will be no record," the Chairman said. "There are no

156

minutes from this meeting. You must follow your orders. Muldowney is to be killed. We expect this to occur as soon as possible, certainly in a matter of hours. He must not fall into the hands of the police. You have got to get to him first."

"We don't want to knew the details."

It was Justice speaking again.

"We just want the matter carried out. It is the best way of resolving the situation, for you as well as the government. You wouldn't want it known outside this room that one of your agents was out of control."

Queally recognized the threat for what it was.

"Very well," he answered in a low voice.

For the present at any rate, he had no option but to agree to what, even in his own highly dissolute interpretation of both law and ethics, was a most dangerous demand.

"Have you any further information about the bullion," the Justice minister asked.

Queally was about to tell them that Muldowney was close behind the conspirators when he checked himself. In the light of the circumstances it would have been foolish to continue. If the Committee believed that Muldowney himself was a primary organizer of the bullion steal, there was no point in telling them that he was hot on the trail of the conspirators.

"O'Connor made contact with an official of the German Embassy," he said, deciding to offer some crumbs of information without revealing their source. He would have very little chance of career redemption if he told them that it was Muldowney who was carrying out the surveillance.

157

"He took away some papers. We don't know what they were about. He deposited them in a left luggage office and posted the ticket to an accommodation address."

He was stuck again. He couldn't tell them that Muldowney had outwitted him by giving him a false address and that their surveillance of the stations had yielded no result.

"We have a problem, however. We don't know where the ticket went, or the station that the documents were deposited in."

He decided to pitch a ball at the ministers.

"Correctly we should open all the bags in the stations," he said. "But this could be dangerous. There could be complaints from the public. It would take a great deal of time to search every piece of luggage in every station. Someone is bound to kick up about it."

"What are you going to do then," the Chairman demanded in exasperation.

Queally thought for a moment.

"Our best course is to see if any of the attendants recognize O'Connor from his description or a photograph and try and identify whatever he left there."

"How important are these documents," one of the other ministers asked.

Queally thought for a moment or two.

"My belief is that the German handed over documents which will allow the conspirators to claim the gold and dispose of it," he said. "Unfortunately we don't know who has the ticket now. If O'Connor is dead we can't ask him" he added sardonically.

"It's quite obvious," the senior minister responded shortly. "It was sent to Muldowney. O'Connor was killed to close off that loophole. Muldowney has either already collected the documents himself or has sent someone else to do so. You're obviously too far behind," he snapped in a sudden rush of anger at the incompetence of the spymaster.

Queally said nothing. He, of course, knew that if Muldowney was part of this he wouldn't have reported the transfer of the papers from the German Embassy in the first place. He fully understood why his subordinate had given him the runaround about the address. He didn't want to be picked up by the police. Queally knew enough about his man to know that the Committee's summation of the situation was totally off key. But at the same time he didn't understand the agent's link with the other two killings.

It seemed as if Muldowney really was part of the plot. But if so why had he tipped Queally off in the first place. The spymaster and his Section would have known nothing about it without Muldowney's initial reports. He looked down at the enlarged photograph of his assistant and stared curiously at the paper which he was holding in his hands. Muldowney was holding as if he wanted it to be photographed as well. The police had concentrated on blowing up the face in the pictures not on what the agent had in his hands. He said nothing, put the pictures in his pocket and got up.

"Kill him," the senior minister reiterated.

He looked around the table at the others. Two of them nodded in acquiescence. The other three said nothing but refused to meet his eye.

159

Queally didn't really believe what he was hearing.

"That is an official government order?" he queried.

The Chairman almost spat out a confirmatory yes. The meeting was over.

Queally went back to his office in a daze. He didn't know how to handle this situation. His career over the years had been one of half truths, embellished non events, sometimes indeed impinging on elements of criminal activity, more often than not reporting on some white collar half hearted attempt to defraud the state with illegal imports of one commodity or another, or the channeling of funds to secret bank accounts overseas. Queally's duties lay more often in the gathering and recording of the improper adventures and perversions of people who might someday have to be importuned to agree to particular decisions.

Violence, it was true, had sometimes occurred, but never had the spymaster been instructed to go out and kill a citizen. He sat in his office, forbidding anyone to enter and thought it all through. There was a time, he knew, in a more violent era, in the early days of the state, when such decisions were taken. Men who were a threat to the public good were quietly warned off, and he had no doubt if they failed to heed that warning were summarily disposed of.

But now there was a judiciary, indeed an eminent judiciary, a reasonably sound police force, a state struggling to make its way in the world, but one which already had enormous international credibility. He realized, of course, that governments from time to time had to take unsavoury decisions, or thought they had. If men could not be trammeled with fitted up crimes and jail sentences then it was likely that there existed a particular clandestine department of state which would undertake the final decision.

Queally shivered. He had suddenly come face to face with a grim reality. He ran that department. He was the man who had to undertake unlicensed killings for which there were no warrants of execution, but which nonetheless had to be carried out as efficiently as if they were the result of judicial process.

He spread the prints he had been given by the ministers out on top of his desk. He looked again at the small white sheets which Muldowney was holding up in front of his chest. He lifted the telephone and asked to be put on to an assistant commissioner in the Phoenix Park depot. The police contact accepted Queally's instructions. He was the officer appointed to liaise between the Section and the ordinary rungs of the police command. The plates were dispatched immediately to Queally's office.

He sent for Cronin. The big man came in quietly sensing that things were not well in Queally's empire. The spymaster told him about the death of O'Connor, and instructed him to stay at his desk all night if necessary in case Muldowney rang in. he said nothing to him about the Cabinet's linking of Muldowney with O'Connor's death. Nor did he do anything about putting the railway stations under surveillance. He didn't have the manpower. If he was right Muldowney already had the documents in his possession. The photographs would soon prove this one way or the other.

When the plates arrived he sent them out to a photographic studio that often carried out contracts for the Section and had plates and prints back an hour later. He locked the glass plates in his safe and spread the prints which now had focused on the white sheets which Muldowney was holding. The enlargements were perfect. He could quite clearly decipher the wording. There was one item in particular which he studied more closely. It was the account identification number from the bank in Switzerland which would allow the holder to reclaim the bullion.

He turned over the other prints and read them closely, but gained little real information. They were copies of consignment dockets and were of little value other than to establish the actual paper trail which the bullion had followed. One of them, however, he studied a little longer. It was a copy of the original instruction to the Central Bank to move the gold. Yet it too gave little information. He had already identified the official who was the source of the original order. Like Muldowney he puzzled over the list of names and dates but like the agent failed to decide just what it was.

His mind went back to the meeting earlier. The Finance minister, Finucane, had been called to the security meeting. Nothing strange about that, after all he had authorized the original movement of the gold to London. Queally pondered things for a moment or two and then checked with Cronin that Muldowney had not made contact, and unlocking the communicating door in his office went into the room next door. It was, as office gossip had surmised, a bedroom, although sparsely furnished. He lay down on the bed and tried to compose his fevered brain.

He faced an incredible dilemma. In his heart he knew that Muldowney was innocent of complicity in the bullion plot. It was highly unlikely that he would have killed anyone either. But there was no doubt that the agent had got close to the heart of the conspiracy. The photographs showed that somehow he had been able to at least scrutinize the documents which formed the bullion's paper trail. If he had been part of the conspiracy he surely would not have been photographing the evidence.

Queally knew he couldn't bring Muldowney in unless he agreed. But the agent as far as he knew was in hiding only because he thought he would be turned over to the police for a murder which he didn't commit. Now there was a darker, more dangerous turn of events. The secret agent didn't know it

162

but he was a dead man if Queally carried out his orders. And if he did, Queally was certain he was destroying the one operative who could help him solve the mystery.

But events had moved on for Queally too. Since being given the awful order to terminate his own assistant, it now appeared that Queally himself might know where the bullion was. The documents had revealed the existence of the Swiss bank. He had no way of getting the gold released. He needed the original deposit and banking orders for that, but he was now one step ahead of the Security Committee. Once more he could go to them and claim his rightful position as the mainstream controller of intelligence which had taken him years to achieve.

His thoughts returned again to the execution order. To carry it out he had to find Muldowney, an apparently impossible task. The odds, the spymaster realized, were more in favour of the police picking him up than on Queally himself locating him.

There was more at stake than Muldowney's guilt or innocence. The Grim Grey Men had made their position clear. Queally could accept that there were other issues, matters involving the financial security of the state which made Muldowney a very minor player in these affairs. But he had become a major burden on the spymaster. Queally had been given a direct order from the Security Committee. Failure to carry it out could have serious repercussions for Queally himself. His career might suddenly be terminated and the years which he had spent contriving his own particular space in the bureaucracy of the nation would be wasted.

Queally was a soulless man. He had no moral difficulty about ordering Muldowney's execution. The thought did not repulse him. Certainly he had never had to accept such a duty before, but the thought that he should raise a moral objection did not occur to him. His future would be determined by his carrying out of his orders. And carry them out he would.

He went back into his office, rested a little, but was not refreshed. He needed to put the arrangements in place even though Muldowney had not yet surfaced. He rang an internal number and contacted the post office security department which had a few days earlier provided Muldowney with the truck for the bullion. Its head was not as highly graded as Queally and did not practice the same philosophy of power through intelligence gathering, but it was here that many of the state's more shameful missions were carried out.

Just as Queally had located his intelligence gathering operation in the shelter of the GPO, so too had the authorities set up this parallel and equally circumspect department, concealing it in the cumbersome sprawl of the system which managed the country's mail and telephone lines. This was where telephone tapping instructions were carried out on behalf of the police, where letter interception orders were sent, where attempts by criminals to subvert the mail were circumvented, but where other darker activities were carried out in the guise of state security.

While Queally supposedly specialized in high grade intelligence work that gave him access to the highest echelons of government, the department presided over by Jack "Gunsmoke" Reynolds, a former prime minister's bodyguard, wallowed in daily trivia. But Reynolds had not been lightly put into his post. He carried out other special assignments from time to time. He had all the connections necessary to find the men who would carry out Queally's deadly mission. Queally knew that Reynolds would not have such men in full time employment, but contracts would go out, secret briefings would be held, and if all went well the Security Committee's dreadful command would be implemented successfully.

His opposite number listened carefully to Queally's guarded

instructions. Special operatives would be on standby until Muldowney surfaced. Queally urged caution. If there was no alternative, Muldowney could be shot or manually killed. If at all possible, however, his death should appear to be an accident.

Queally knew that no matter how determined the ministers were to have their orders carried out, they would not welcome an untidy operation. The last thing they wanted was a high profile assassination.

Chapter Twelve

Muldowney went into the reading room of one of the city's public libraries. It gave him shelter, warmth and a distance from the crowded streets and time to allow him to consider his next move. He was in a state of shock after the death of the photographer. He knew nothing of the death of O'Connor but even at this stage he realized that if the police connected him with that death, matters would become very serious. An all out manhunt would undoubtedly ensure.

He reviewed his options. While Finucane had succeeded in getting hold of the original documents, Muldowney had managed to get copies made. He was satisfied that they were in a safe place. This would surely give him enough leverage to make Queally accept that the photographers death was accidental and did not call for any prosecution of his agent. In this way Muldowney was certain he could be left out of the picture.

For a moment he wondered about the mysterious man whose body had been found with the brass ingots. He puzzled over this again for a while but once more dismissed the matter. It was just coincidence, he persuaded himself. For all that was known he might just have been a passerby who had a heart attack.

He decided that his best move was to contact the spymaster again, identify the Finance minister and produce his evidence, subject to assurances that the issue of the photographer's death would be buried with him. Muldowney knew that MI6 or the CIA would have no difficulty with such a scenario. They would send in their cleaners and the whole situation would just vanish.

He went outside to find a telephone to call in and caught the raucous cry of an early evening newsboy. He bought the paper and scanned its pages. At first he thought it was the dead photographer who had made the headlines. He nearly collapsed when he read the opening black type paragraphs of the lead story. It reported O'Connor's death from heart failure after a raid by an intruder. The details were sketchy but other than to say that the soldier had been tied up in his own house, there was little more hard information.

Even in his now highly unbalanced state Muldowney could read between the lines. The authorities had moved to keep the real story under wraps. For a moment he gave thanks that Queally in his own domain was just as powerful and farseeing as MI6 or the CIA. He hadn't been able to close down the whole story, but at least he had kept his agent's role out of it, he reasoned. Little did he know that Queally had known nothing about the soldier's death until the Grim Grey Men had imparted the news at the Security Committee meeting. It was the Security Committee not the spymaster which was managing events.

He read the piece to the end and then roamed over the rest of the paper. There was no mention of the photographer at all. Either the body had not been found or Queally had been able to move much more quickly on that particular problem.

Muldowney was almost reeling with the shock and the disturbing impact of it all. He put out a hand and steadied himself at a lamp post. He set off again, stumbling blindly along the street, crashing into people coming in the opposite direction, drawing the ire of some and the revulsion of others who immediately assumed that he was drunk. The back of his head was pounding, huge hammer blows beating against the inside of his skull. Finally he realized that he must get himself in check but by then it seemed that madness had truly engulfed him.

He was back in Dame street again. Suddenly a horde of shouting gesticulating people rushed from the doors of the

Olympia Theatre. They ran out into the street, causing the traffic to come to a halt. They peered under cars and buses, running from one to the other, stooping over and searching the ground around and under each vehicle.

There were at least two dozen of these extraordinary searching people, men and women, all of them calling out as if hailing some missing comrade, totally ignoring the traffic and the passers by. Crowds began to gather on either side of the street as the seekers ran up and down. Traffic braked to a halt.

Muldowney stared at them in crazed agony. His mind had broken down he thought. These people were fellow sufferers. He pushed through the crowds and ran out into the street to join the berserk band of seeking people. He caught one woman by the arm.

"What are you looking for?" he asked.

She pushed past him and went up to another car and looked inside first and then went down on her knees to see if there was anything underneath it.

A couple of exasperated policemen were trying to control the situation, stopping the traffic to prevent the frantic seekers form being run over. The crowds on the footpath began to cheer as the people pursued their hunt. Then suddenly as if each had received some secret instant command all of them stopped their excited chase and walked off as if nothing had happened.

Muldowney leaned weakly against a street bollard trying to get a grip on himself. What was happening to him. A bystander turned to him, a huge grin of enjoyment spread right across his face.

"He's done it every day this week.   A great bloody show it is.

Looking for leprechauns. What will he think up next!"

He jerked his head at the theatre doorway. Muldowney walked up to look at the billboard.

A well known hypnotist was on stage this week. Then Muldowney understood what had happened. The seekers had been hypnotised on the stage and sent out into the streets to hunt for the leprechauns. It was a spectacular if unorthodox piece of showmanship. When the effects of the hypnosis wore off they went home no the wiser.

Muldowney laughed, a long loud foolish laugh of relief and tried to pull himself together. He rapidly reviewed his options. There were in reality only two. He could either stay out of contact or report in. He decided to reconnect to the Section. Irrespective of O'Connor's death which Queally would obviously connect to the agent and that of the camera man which he might not, Muldowney reckoned he had something to bargain with. He had the name of the minister involved and the photographs of the documents to back up his claim. What he didn't know, of course, was that Queally too had prints from the dead man's plates.

He rang in and got through to Queally.

"I'll send Cronin to pick you up," the spymaster said. "Where are you now."

Muldowney told him and Queally directed him to walk on and meet Cronin in the older part of the city. He gave his agent a meeting point near St Patrick's Cathedral and telephoned Reynolds in post office security. After a few moments discussion he put down the telephone and sent for Cronin.

"You're to pick up Muldowney and bring him to the Black Horse at Inchicore. I'll meet you there."

The only reasons he gave the Black Horse as a meeting place was that it was still in his mind as the location of his encounter with his subordinate two nights previously.

"We're to meet Queally at the pub near Inchicore," Cronin told Muldowney when he settled into the car.

Muldowney saw no reason to disbelieve him. The familiarity of the location gave him a renewed sense of confidence. He filled his colleague in on some of the events of the past forty eight hours, gave him the background to the soldier's death. He told him about the death of the photographer as well.

"There's nothing in the paper about that," he said to Cronin when he had finished.

The big man pursed his lips.

Queally knows about it," he said. "I heard him talking to the police, but they're keeping it quiet for some reason."

Muldowney cheered up a bit at this information. It was obvious now that Queally had gone into a damage limitation exercise. He would be kept out of the hands of the police.

The big man stopped at traffic lights and cursed as a postal lorry heavily laden with huge coils of wire on wooden reels shot past them and dropped gears and speed to get up the hill. Cronin slowed down a bit to allow the truck some space. Muldowney shifted uneasily in his seat. Some deep seated instinct sounded a warning. He looked ahead at the truck and actually saw the first of two wooden reels of wire fall over its tailboard and come trundling down the street towards them.

He shouted at Cronin. The big man stared frozenly at the huge rolling killer coils. Almost at the last minute he swung the steering wheel and avoided the reel by inches. The big man went to pull up but Muldowney stopped him.

"Drive on, drive on," he shouted. "It's a trap. They're after me."

Cronin responded instinctively to his shouts and put his foot down accelerating past the lorry. It had come to a halt and two overalled men were getting out of the cab. A third man was standing in the back staring down at his lost cargo. Muldowney looked back. There was a crash, the first of the huge reels had hit a car behind and smashed it into a lampost. Someone had to be hurt but Muldowney's response was clearcut.

"Drive on, drive on," he urged the big man. Obediently Cronin put down his foot and they took off as quickly as possible.

Half a mile away Cronin brought the car to the kerb. He switched off the ignition and turned to Muldowney.

"You can take the car," he said. "I'm getting out. I don't know what this is all about, but I would have been killed along with you."

Muldowney nodded in agreement. He was less shaken than his colleague. The ongoing trauma of the past three days had suddenly uncovered a new, previously unrevealed, source of strength. It was as if he were outside the whole scenario looking in. Cronin sat motionless in the driver's seat.

"Queally sent me out to be killed," he said. "I just don't believe it."

"You've been set up," Muldowney said. "Just like me. That business with the body and the brass bars. That was some sort of a frame up to incriminate you."

171

The big man was silent. Muldowney asked him if there was any more information on the identity of the corpse. Cronin shook his head.

"Nothing," he said. "Nothing at all."

"Where does Queally fit into all this" Muldowney asked Cronin.

The big man thought for a moment.

"He's in at the heart of it," he said. "He takes his orders from the government. Whatever this is all about goes really high up."

Muldowney silently agreed with him. He knew just how high up it went and the name of the minister who had organized the bullion shipment in the first place, but now he wondered if there were others involved. He was sure that Queally would not have tried to assassinate him off his own bat. He would have to have been given instructions by someone. Perhaps Finucane had organized this attempted murder. His head began to spin again. Finucane seemed a very likely candidate. From his standpoint, with Muldowney out of the way, there was no evidence against him. He had recovered the papers and was not to know that Muldowney had made copies.

But it was the spymaster who had set up the meeting and arranged for Cronin to collect him. He raced over the facts again. No one else knew that he would be in the car with Cronin. But why try to kill Cronin as well, unless it would give some sort of cover to his own assassination. Or perhaps they thought that Cronin really was a part of the conspiracy, or perhaps knew more than was apparent. Muldowney didn't know which solution to go for, but now fine tuned to the disturbing complexities of the situation recognized the need to become invisible once more.   He knew what action he had to take.

His companion was still slumped in front of the steering wheel. He shook him and the big man slowly turned to him.

"You can do two things," Muldowney told him. "You can stay with me, or you can go and take your chances on your own."

The big man licked his lips. He was still white faced and in shock. An expression of plaintive indecision crossed his face and he stared helplessly at Muldowney.

"I don't know," he said. "I don't know. I just followed my orders. It's you they're after."

"Make up your mind," Muldowney said roughly. "Either stay or go."

The big man got slowly out of the car. Muldowney slipped across the front seat and took the steering wheel. Cronin leaned in through the open driver's window.

"What will I do," he asked.

Muldowney started the ignition.

"Lose yourself," he urged. "Get out of sight, go home, go to England. Anything. Whatever you do, don't go back in."

Muldowney drove off. His last glimpse of the big man as to see him still standing on the pavement, a big rumpled mass of indecision.

Muldowney drove on and tried to sort out his next move. In a way, Cronin's flight, if he carried it through, was to his advantage. Queally now had to deal with two of his agents on the loose and dangerous.

173

He smiled grimly at his analysis of the spymaster's difficulty. His murder attempt had failed. Muldowney was still free and as far as he, knew had more cards to play in terms of information than the spymaster. At the very least he had evidence which would expose a senior member of the government and perhaps others, if it was brought into the light of day. That evidence would give the secret agent the foundations of a defence to whatever charges might be brought against him. In his heart of course Muldowney knew that there would never be any charges. He would be killed for what he knew. That was obvious now.

This analysis of just where he stood hit him a sickening blow inside. He tried to rationalize his situation with the pretext that it was all part and parcel of being a secret agent, but his brain told him at the same time that matters had gone over the top. However, he was a little bit safer now that he had started running a decoy. If Cronin was any use at all he would keep the police and the security people tied up while Muldowney himself dealt with the serious issues which no confronted him.

Unconsciously he headed out towards the suburbs again. He was better off being mobile but he knew it was only a matter of time before the car's number and description would be in the hands of the police. However, he reasoned, it would be some hours yet before the fact that Cronin had gone on the run as well as Muldowney got through to the Section, although he was sure that by now whoever had ordered the murder attempt had already received the news that if had failed. What was he to do. The whole scene was fraught with difficulty. It was imperative that he should not make any mistakes. One wrong move and he was doomed. Under no circumstances could he be caught.

The agent decided his best move now was to reconnect with Finucane. There was only one way to do that and that was to go back to Joyce Dolan's house. He parked the Section car in the rear lane and went through the back garden as he had done before. The cellar door was still open and he was inside in seconds.

They were both in the front room. Finucane sprang to his feet in alarm as he burst in. The woman sat apparently unperturbed although he could see a look of apprehension in her eyes.

"Sit down," he ordered the minister.

He crossed to the window and looked outside. The black state car with its detective driver was parked in the street. He turned around to face Finucane.

"I want you to be very clear about something," he said. "I have enough evidence to put you in jail."

Finucane almost sneered at him.

"You're the one that's going to jail," he countered. "The whole country is looking for you."

Muldowney smiled a wooden fixed smile that conveyed little mirth but great understanding.

"That may be so," he said. "But a few people will be going with me and you are one of them."

"They're going to kill you," the minister burst out. "The Security Committee ordered it this morning. You've killed three people."

"Two," Muldowney corrected. "And both of them were accidental deaths."

"The police say its murder," Finucane said.

175

He was staring at Muldowney, fearful that he was confronted by a madman who might all of a sudden leap across the room and attack him.

Muldowney digested this new piece of information.

"The government are trying to kill me," he said incredulously.

Finucane repeated. "The Security Committee gave the order today."

Muldowney was stunned. He could half accept that the plotters might want to have him eliminated, but the government. This was something else. He was their man, their loyal servant, only trying to do his job.

"They've already tried and failed," he said eventually. "But some innocent motorists and his family may have been killed or badly injured. I am still alive and very, very dangerous."

He slammed the words through his teeth at the minister who recoiled slightly and then recovered his composure. There was a new dimension emerging to Muldowney. Finucane even at this stage could see that the agent had developed from a vacuous naïve fool into a sharpened dangerous operative who was becoming more and more fine honed as events moved on.

He sat down in the chair.

Joyce spoke for the first time.

"Would you like some tea, a drink?"

She got up and went to leave the room. Muldowney ordered her back to her seat.

"Stay where you are. I'll have something later."

176

"I want to know more about this Security Committee meeting," he said to Finucane.

The minister was already weighing up his situation. The plausibility and articulate skills of the politician always ready to think on his feet were coming to the fore.

"The Security committee is dealing with the bullion issue," he said. "I am not a member," he admitted, "but I was there to report on my Department's part in the gold transfer."

"Just what was your department's role," Muldowney demanded.

Finucane was silent for a moment.

"We organized the commercial arrangements in conjunction with the Central Bank," he said. "It was a joint operation."

"You have got hold of the wrong end of the stick about this," the minister went on, deciding that he should take every opportunity possible to reshape the agent's assessment of the situation. "The bullion was moved on government orders. I know that. I signed the requisition."

Muldowney interrupted.

"I was down at the Central Bank. The government didn't authorize the last leg of the journey. The bullion was diverted to Frankfurt and then to a Swiss bank."

The minister swallowed uncomfortably and tried to regain the higher ground of is narrative.

"I was acting for the Security Committee," he said. "They made the decision. There was a numbered account. The bullion was to be paid out from Switzerland. It was a trick to foil the currency speculators."

The politician then decided to go on the attack.

"You on the other hand are a complete fantasist. You made up this yarn about a conspiracy in the civil service, brought it to your department and caused the deaths of innocent people. The Committee believes you are insane and you are to be hunted down and killed. Those are the orders. Your boss Queally has been instructed to carry them out."

Muldowney now had Queally's involvement in the murder attempt confirmed. It was no consolation to him.

"Why are people trying to kill me instead of arresting me," he demanded.

Finucane had his answer ready.

"There are times when the state runs up against madmen who are too dangerous and too clever for the police," he said. "Then we have to take special steps to deal with special situations. This is one of those situations."

Muldowney nodded his acceptance of what the minister said. He too had read accounts in the newspapers from time to time of unexplained shootings by G men and Special branch officers. Suspects had been killed in the course of capture.

Finucane's confirmation of the situation was only shocking to him in so far as it disclosed that the order to kill him had come from such a high source. He quickly reviewed the rest of what Finucane had told him. The minister was plausible, even convincing, but Muldowney believed he had already put the blame for the matter squarely where it belonged. Finucane was part of a plot to defraud the state, he was certain. The question was how many others were involved and would he survive to reveal the truth and clear his name.

"I intend to follow this whole thing through to the end," Muldowney told the minister. "You are one of the guilty men. I want to know who the others are."

Finucane all but laughed in his face.

"I have only to throw something through the window and there will be an armed detective in here in seconds," he said. "Have you got a gun," he challenged.

Muldowney made no reply. He wasn't going to regurgitate Queally's comment that untrained men couldn't have weapons. The more dangerous he appeared to be to Finucane the better.

He turned to Joyce.

"Go out to the far and tell the driver that he can go for the night," he ordered. "If you do anything more than that I'll kill both of you before they can get inside."

The woman changed colour and walking quickly and silently left the room. He went to the window and watched her go down the steps and talk to the driver. Moments later the car engine started and the vehicle purred away. She came back inside.

"You can make us some food," he told her. "Malachy and I are going to have a talk."

She hesitated and he smiled slightly at her as a form of reassurance.

"Don't worry," he said. "I'm not going to hurt him."

179

She went to the kitchen and Muldowney helped himself to a drink from the cabinet. He offered Finucane something but the minister refused. He was watchful now, cautious, realizing that his attempts to play on the secret agent's gullibility had not succeeded. Had they met before this whole episode, while Muldowney was still basking in the euphoria of his glamorous if uneventful life, it might have been a different story. Finucane was an adept practitioner of expressing conviction and assurance. He knew how to handle men. He had still to get the secret agent's measure and he could only wait and see what Muldowney next proposed.

Muldowney in fact had nothing to propose. He scowled into his drink searching for guidance. As far as a plan of action was concerned he was virtually at a dead end. Paradoxically it now seemed that his salvation lay in the hands of the politician whom he considered a criminal and the author of a large part of his misfortune. On the other hand Queally too was a direct instigator of many of his tribulations. It was Queally who was the real fantasist, he decided. It was Queally who had set up this extraordinary clandestine department with its secret officials which functioned outside the normal institutions of the state. It was Queally who had for years survived on whimsical tales and half truths of imaginary conspiracies and wrongdoing, prying into people's lives and disseminating information which could be used by their political and business enemies.

In a sudden impulse he got up, walked out to the phone in the hall and telephoned the spymaster. Queally as he had expected was alone in his office.

"You bastard," he half shouted down the phone at the surprised spymaster. "I'm on to you. You tried to have me killed. I know all about it and I'm going after you and the government."

180

He hung up satisfied that the call would have concluded before Queally would have had any opportunity to have it traced. Then he went back into the front room and the man whom he had to bring down to clear his name.

Joyce served a buffet from a trolley and they ate in their chairs. The woman turned on a wireless to catch the evening news and they listened to a report of the serious accident near St Patrick's Cathedral involving a family car and a dislodged load. Two people had been seriously injured and were in hospital. The station didn't disclose the information that the lorry was from the postal service. That was not surprising since it was the postal service which also controlled the broadcasting system.

Muldowney brought out a pencil and paper and looked across at the minister.

"I want the names of the ministers on this committee," he said.

He wrote them down as Finucane called out the names. Defence, Justice, External Affairs, a junior minister who represented a busy premier and a senior civil servant who acted as permanent secretary. Finucane said again that he had been there that morning because of the specific enquiry about the bullion. As Finance minister he was not a Security Committee member and did not usually attend meetings.

Muldowney pored over the list. These were the men who had ordered his death. The vote had apparently been unanimous. It seemed logical that amongst them were other conspirators.

Finucane read his thoughts.

"There is no point in you going to see these men," he said. "You won't get near them."

181

"I got to you," Muldowney rejoined. "If I could do that I can get to these people."

Finucane was silent. The secret agent had got his thrust home. Had indeed got to Finucane. He suddenly understood again that this man was not perhaps the fool that he had originally taken him for.

"There is another way," he said. "You have no chance on your own. This is way above your head. Nothing that was done in connection with the bullion has been done for private gain. The interests of the country are at stake."

He started to explain the ramifications of the bullion transaction, how underground international speculators were moving against the country undermining its reserves, pressurizing it out of the international money market. The Security Committee had decided that there was only one way out of the problem. It had to buy them off. The bullion was the blackmail money. They were using it as bait, hoping that the speculators would be caught before they had succeeded in moving it out of the Swiss bank. What he didn't say was that the decision should have been one for the full Cabinet. The Security Committee had given itself powers which it did not possess.

Muldowney listened in silence. He was almost convinced by Finucane's tale. A lot of it was probably true. Certainly it purported to re-establish a belief in the integrity of the men of government, although it did nothing to overcome his personal enmity of the Grim Grey Men who had ordered his execution.

"Your best course of action," Finucane urged, "is to joined up with me. I will keep you under wraps and when the emergency is over I can explain the circumstances to the Security Committee and let you off the hook."

Muldowney decided to go along with the proposal for the present. He was tired now. The rapid surge of events were taking its toll of his strength. They agreed that he should remain in Joyce Dolan's house. The minister would send his car for him tomorrow and he would be brought to his department where they would decide what steps to take.

Muldowney agreed. The minister went to the phone to recall his car. The agent glanced at Joyce. The woman was regarding him sympathetically.

"Malachy will sort everything out," she said kindly. "He's a very good man. You can rely on him."

He went up to his room, worn out and worrying about whether or not he had made the right decision. Somehow he felt as if he had been disarmed, as if some of the strength which he had gained from his hold over the Finance minister had been dispelled. Once again he had felt himself vulnerable, exposed. His safety now lay in the hands of the suspect minister whose state car was now winging him homewards across the city. How could be, Muldowney, a lowly civil servant, inexperienced in the wiles of government, without power or influence, already seriously compromised, possibly hope to come out on top.

Chapter Thirteen

The banker Rodgers, and Dalton, the senior civil servant were in Finucane's office when Muldowney went there the following morning. The Finance minister's state car had arrived for him promptly and he was inside government buildings within half an hour. Muldowney had half expected that Queally would be present but there was no sign of the spymaster. Finucane sat behind his desk. The others hovered nervously around the empty fireplace. Muldowney sat upright in an office chair. He was the most outwardly calm of them all, but inside he was electric with his resolve to apprehend these men.

Finucane summarized the situation, making it clear that all three of them had followed instructions. The Cabinet had authorized the shipment of gold to London in the belief that they were taking the pressure off the Irish currency. It was normal defensive procedure. The Security Committee decided that the bullion was to be secretly re-directed to Switzerland and the speculators unmasked as they endeavoured to seize it. The plan had come apart. The gold had vanished. No one knew who had stolen it.

Muldowney listened in silence.

"What you are saying," he said, "is that our Section found out about this transaction, put a wrong interpretation on events, and have been looking for a conspiracy amongst Irish officials where none existed."

Finucane agreed.

"If this is the case, then why did the bullion not arrive at its proper destination," Muldowney demanded.

"We are just as concerned about this as you are," Rodgers spoke for the first time. "Somewhere, either in London or on the Continent the gold was stolen. That's all we know."

"It's in another Swiss bank or some bunker in Germany," Muldowney said coldly.

Finucane shook his head.

"It isn't," he said. "The gold went missing in Frankfurt. There have been no bullion arrivals in Switzerland. My department checked with the Swiss authorities."

"We have a crisis on our hands" Rodgers intervened. "The bullion is definitely missing. We don't know what to do next."

The banker was obviously distraught. It was clear that he too was mystified. Finucane's disclose about the gold being lost in Frankfurt had upset him. He had not known this until now.

Muldowney stared at Finucane. The man's face was its usual inscrutable mask. The agent thought things over very carefully. Then he began to see some daylight. Perhaps only two of his suspects were criminals. He was now certain that the official Dalton was innocent. There was something about the banker, Rodgers, that made him doubtful. But the situation was now much more clear. Finucane and the German embassy official Mannheim were key players.

Finucane had put the gold in play, the German attaché had the connections and the authority to engineer its disappearance. Mannheim's documents were being brought to Finucane by O'Connor so that the Finance minister could show that the bullion had been sent to the Swiss bank as arranged. Because of Muldowney's hue and cry, however, the real situation had been disclosed prematurely. The Security Committee now knew that the gold was missing. Finucane was covering his tracks by allowing Muldowney to investigate. Only he and Mannheim really knew what had happened to the bullion.

Muldowney took further stock of the situation. He had been deliberately presented to Finucane's colleagues as the man who was investigating the disappearance of the bullion. That Muldowney was in fact a wanted man, was under sentence of death by the Security Committee, was a secret which had been kept from the other two. Muldowney could see now what Finucane was up to. He could stop these two men from going to the Security Commitee by putting Muldowney on to them as the official investigator. It was a neat piece of work.

The secret agent decided to go along with events. If it suited Finucane to conceal the fact that Muldowney was a fugitive from the Security Committee, that too suited the agent. Finucane obviously felt that Muldowney under his hand was a safer option than Muldowney loose in the city running his own operation. The officials were also kept in check by the arrangement. It was a classic exercise in duplicity.

The revelation that the gold sent covertly to Switzerland had in fact never arrived was a stunning twist to the saga. The scenario was becoming more and more complicated. The secret agent was rapidly becoming overwhelmed with the ramifications of the affair. Was Finucane really innocent, or was he even more devious than he had seemed at first, or were there other so far unidentified conspirators involved. He abandoned his thoughts and glanced around the group. They were waiting expectantly for a declaration of intent.

"All I can do, gentlemen, is to follow up all the leads I can get," he said.

Finucane interjected.

"He will work out of my Department," he said, "and co-ordinate all the reports and information from the other security agencies."

186

The others left satisfied that they were up to speed on all developments.

"This is a high risk strategy," Muldowney told the minister. "If they get together with the Security ministers at a meeting it will come out that Queally is running the investigation and that I am being hunted for murder."

"You'll have to take your chances," Finucane said. "Keeping those two quiet will give you some time to clear things up."

"I'm not so sure that I shouldn't go to Queally and give him the full information," Muldowney said.

"You're being sought for two and possibly three killings,' Finucane responded. "You will have to keep as far away as possible from Queally."

"What happens if I'm identified," Muldowney asked. "Every policeman in Dublin must be looking for me by now."

"They won't keep up that kind of pressure," Finucane countered. "Queally knows now that the attempt to kill you went wrong and that Cronin will have turned against him as well. They won't want you to end up in the hands of the police. You know too much. They'll have to hunt you down privately. And for the moment you're ahead of them. They've taken their crack at you and failed."

"Those two officials know my name," Muldowney argued referring to the departed civil servant and the banker. "Even though they're not on the Security Committee they might hear about me from other ministers. They could give me away."

Finucane shook his head.

187

"No chance," he said laconically. "No one on the Committee is going to talk about you or about having given orders to have you killed. You're safe enough for the moment."

Muldowney thought it over. Finucane was installing him in his own Department ostensibly to find out what happened to the bullion. It was a bluff. Muldowney was not totally convinced that the politician and the German diplomat knew exactly where the gold was. The problem was he couldn't prove anything. All the evidence he had merely amounted to proof that Finucane had done what he was supposed to do, which was to ship the gold to the Swiss bank. He had no proof that Finucane was actually responsible for its disappearance.

Muldowney studied his rival for a few moments. He had no evidence of anything, but his instincts still told him that he was correct. This was a very devious man. Proving his duplicity was going to be very difficult indeed.

He decided to have a go at Finucane from another angle.

"The body that was found with the brass bars," he said. "That has to be investigated. There's a tie up somewhere."

Finucane threw his arms open in exasperation.

"No one knows who he is or why he was killed."

"My rival investigators will be concentrating on the other two deaths," Muldowney commented thoughtfully. "I know that they were accidental but they will keep people occupied for the moment. I think I'll try to develop some leads from the killing on the building site."

There was no sign of concern on Finucane's face when he outlined his intentions.

"How will you follow it up," he asked curiously. "You'll need connections in the police."

Muldowney nodded.

"That's right," he said. "I have my own contacts there. I'll need that office," he went on. "I need to work in private."

Finucane pressed a buzzer and an official knocked discreetly and came into the room.

"This man will be working with me for a few days," he said. "Get him an office on this floor and anything else he needs."

He turned to the agent.

"Are you going back to Rathgar tonight."

Muldowney thought for a moment.

"Yes,' he said. "It's safe there. I need somewhere to stay."

"I'll ring Joyce and arrange that," the minister said.

Another official came into the office carrying files. Finucane dismissed the agent. The business of the day was beginning, and murder, bullion or whatever, affairs of state could not be delayed no matter what other pressures were on a minister.

Muldowney followed the official to an office and called up a direct line from the switchboard. He rang the detective O'Brien. The detective answered him at first in hesitant strangled tones, but finally got overt his surprise.

"I thought you were on the run," he said.

"Don't believe all you hear," Muldowney said.   "It's Cronin they're after not me. I want everything you can get on the body which was found with the brass," he told the detective. "And I want to know what the current situation is about Veronica."

Someone brought him a cup of tea and after an hour or so he rang the detective again.

"The dead man still hasn't been identified," O'Brien told him. "The medical examiner says he was strangled. It would have taken a strong man. It's murder alright."

"Is anything else happening," he asked the detective.

"No," O'Brien said. "But you were right about Cronin. There's an all station bulletin on him. There's no mention of you now at all."

Muldowney felt a sense of satisfaction. Queally had called off his dogs, as Finucane had predicted.

"What about Veronica?"

"She's being brought to court this morning," the detective said. "They're making a case for possession of stolen property. It's a fit up," he said. "The girl did nothing, but they seem to want to put her away for a while for some reason."

Muldowney was concerned.

"Can anything be done about her," he asked.

"They've a strong case," the detective said. "They put some things in her bag, cash and jewelry which had been stolen. She can deny it until she's blue in the face but the evidence will stick. She'll go down, they're determined on it."

THE IRISH SECRET AGENT

"Why?" Muldowney asked.

The detective picked up the concern in his voice and was a little more forthcoming.

"Somebody wants her out of the way for a while," he said. "She knows too much. It's as simple as that."

Muldowney was astounded. His sense of justice had taken a few fairly hard knocks over recent days, but this was just too much altogether.

"She's totally innocent," he said. "She was only following instructions."

"You know that and I know that," the detective said. "But unless you want to go to court and say that, there is nothing that can be done. I certainly am not going to stick my neck out."

"O.K." Muldowney said resignedly. "Leave it with me. I can't do anything at the moment, but I'll get her out in a few days time."

The detective was impressed. His initial concern about being contacted again by the secret agent had been dissipated by the aplomb and efficiency with which he was dealing with things. He was further impressed by the very obvious fact that the secret agent was not in custody and seemed to be fully in charge of matters.

"I'll contact you again," Muldowney told the detective and hung up.

He put his feet up on the desk and folded his hands behind his head, roving over the whole sequence of events in his mind once more. The unidentified body was one clue, but so far it had yielded nothing. O'Connor had been another lead but it had already brought him to Finucane and in any event the army officer too was dead. That left the German. He rationalized the situation further. Mannheim was the key. Finucane organized getting the bullion. Mannheim had disposed of it. If he was able to break down the German he would be able to prove his case against the minister. That was the way forward. Proof of this would reinstate him in his position, establish his innocence and perhaps even open up the route to taking over Queally's job.

Queally in Muldowney's view was now a spent force. The agent felt that he was well ahead. The spymaster was struggling with spent out leads and irrelevant information. But Muldowney realized he still had tremendous power. He apparently controlled assassins who would wipe him out without the slightest compunction. At the same time he decided that Queally was seriously dangerous only if he found out more about the conspiracy than Muldowney himself. For the moment the secret agent had the edge.

Muldowney left the building and took a taxi out to the Embassy. He claimed an appointment with Mannheim and was directed upstairs immediately. Obviously his previous visit had registered with the butler and it was assumed that he was entitled to access. He entered the diplomat's office and stepped back in astonishment and alarm. There were two men inside. One was the attaché, the other was Queally.

Muldowney rapidly processed the implications of this unexpected and extraordinary meeting. He quickly realized that Queally too had worked over the information in his possession and decided that the German was his only lead. The spymaster half rose from his seat.

Muldowney thrust his hand into his right hand jacket pocket and pointing a finger to make a resemblance of a hidden gun,

192

motioned Queally back into his seat. The German seemed surprised for a few seconds, but evidently recognizing his visitor as yet another Irish agent did not seem unduly alarmed. Muldowney came right into the room and closed the door behind him.

The spymaster was agitated. The appearance of his unruly apprentice was the last thing he expected. He glared balefully at the agent, but Muldowney ignored his attitude. He was icily calm now, but his anger at the treachery of his head of Section was tempered with the realization that the way out of his dilemma lay in extracting as much further information from the German as possible.

He decided to bluff the diplomat into believing that he and Queally presented a united front. He glanced at Queally.

"What have you got from him?"

The spymaster was shrewd enough to back his agent's play.

"Nothing more than you already reported," the spymaster answered.

He stared at the German who spread out his hands expressively and asked with a touch of plaintiveness:

"Gentlemen, what more can I tell you."

Muldowney delved deeper.

"The bullion has not reached the Swiss bank," he said. "Where is it now?"

The German made another gesture of ignorance.

"I don't know," he said. "The documentation was all in order.

I gave Colonel O'Connor the complete dossier."

Muldowney wondered if he knew that the soldier was dead but decided to leave that aspect of the issue alone.

"The bullion was diverted from London to Germany as arranged. It vanished in Germany. The Swiss authorities say there were no bullion imports."

The German protested.

"The transfer from London to Frankfurt was carried out at the request of the Irish authorities," he said. "My government knows nothing of what occurred after it left Frankfurt for Switzerland. We were only responsible for shipment to Frankfurt. The gold was put on the train to Switzerland. Our involvement end there."

Muldowney couldn't decide whether to believe the man or not. He turned to Queally.

"What do you make of it?"

The spymaster, his composure totally recovered from his shock at Muldowney's entrance, shook his head.

"I don't know," he confessed. A million pounds of gold bullion cannot vanish into thin air."

Muldowney turned to the German again.

"There must be some record of another route change."

The German shrugged.

"If there was further authorization I know nothing about it. There is no record of any new instructions."
194

"How was the bullion to get from Frankfurt to the bank in Zurich," the spymaster queried.

"By train for most of the journey and then by armed vehicle across the city to the bank."

"Was any escort provided on the train," Muldowney asked.

"The cargo was not identifiable in the overland manifests," the German said. "An escort wasn't considered necessary. We didn't want to draw attention to it. No one knew it was being shipped on from London, except an official from the bank, of course, who traveled with the consignment."

Muldowney was aroused.

"What official," he asked.. "Where did he come into it."

The German opened his hands expressively again.

"From the British bank," he said. "He travelled with the shipment from Dublin."

Mukldowney looked at the spymaster.

"He did not," he said emphatically. "I went with the bullion from the Central Bank to Baldonnel airport. No civilian official went with it."

The German seemed perturbed for a moment or so, but then let the point slide away. Bank officials, British or Irish, or indeed German or Swiss, were not his direct concern.

"My only role in this matter, gentlemen, was to smooth the customs arrangements for your government," he said. "I am very concerned that something has gone wrong, but I must also point out that all the necessary arrangements sought were

195

put in place and were followed to the letter."

"Except that the gold never arrived," Muldowney commented.

He jerked his head at Queally.

"We're leaving now," he said.

He kept his hand in his pocket, still simulating the holding of a gun. The spymaster was eyeing the bulge worriedly, but it seemed to have made no impact on the German. Queally shook hands with the now slightly haughty diplomat. Muldowney gave a slight bow unconsciously deciding to imitate the formality and display of Continental manners exhibited by the German and they left.

Queally had a Section car. They got in and sat for a few moments reviewing the conversation in the embassy.

"Well," Muldowney said. "We know now who the unidentified dead man is."

Queally looked at him in astonishment.

"Who?" he asked.

Muldowney told him to drive away before he answered.

"The Bank of England official," he said. "If you check with London you'll find that he hasn't been to his office for a number of days."

"Why weren't we told about this man before,' Queally asked. "Who killed him and why"

The spymaster was annoyed. He had again temporarily lost control of his thought process.

"He was killed to cover up the Security Committee's instructions to re-direct the gold," Muldowney explained. "He knew too much."

He ruminated for a few moments more.

"Rodgers should have told us about him," he went on. "He had to know the man was in Dublin."

"The bank knew about him?" Queally responded in surprise.

Muldowney nodded.

"Of course. Rodgers had to know he was involved. He was sent over from England to check off the serial numbers on the bullion bars or sign manifests or receipts or something."

Queally drove slowly towards Donnybrook. He was now more focused on the agent's explanations and grasped the implications of what Muldowney was saying as quickly as he voiced the thoughts coming into his mind.

"This is getting very serious. Rodgers has questions to answer."

Muldowney agreed.

"Now," he said. "I want some explanations from you."

The car swerved slightly in Queally's suddenly tremulous hands, alarmed with the sudden roughness in the secret agent's voice.

"You tried to get me killed," Muldowney said. "and you almost killed Cronin in the process. I know who gave you the orders, but I want to know why."

"You know about the orders?" Queally echoed incredulously.

"Yes," Muldowney answered, pleased that he was able to hit the spymaster with the information provided by Finucane. "The Security Committee ordered me to be killed and you hired the killers. Very ineffective killers they were too," he added with a show of bitter bravado.

Queally was mesmerized by the fact that Muldowney appeared to be in possession of information which was very top secret indeed.

"How do you know this," he asked Muldowney.

"I have my own channels," the agent said. "I am also aware of the fact that you have been ordered to pull back from me and hunt down Cronin."

"I think Cronin was definitely involved in the killing of the man at the brass dump,' Queally said. "I know you killed O'Connor and the photographer."

Muldowney was startled. It was the first time that the photographer's death had come up.

"It was an accident," he said. "He hit his head when he fell. But how do you know that I am connected with that."

Queally explained that the photographer had included Muldowney's face in the frame when he took the pictures of the documents at the reception. Muldowney whistled softly.

"He wasn't so slow," he said in a flicker of admiration and then dismissed the man from his thoughts altogether. "So you have the photographer's plates," he said to the spymaster.

Queally admitted it.

"What I want to know," he said. "Is where are the originals."

Muldowney said nothing. He knew where they were, in Finucane's hands. But the less Queally knew about the Finance minister for the moment the better.

"They're safe," he said, giving the impression hat he alone was the one who held the documents. He was doubly glad that he had had them copied as personal insurance.

Queally seemed satisfied, but the news that the spymaster had the plates disturbed Muldowney. Up to now he had thought that he held a strong hand, that the evidence he held could prove his innocence. Now Queally had copies too. However, he didn't see that this could do him any immediate harm.

"We're missing the key piecc of information," he said. "We don't know where the gold is and who is responsible for its disappearance."

"It's definitely not in the bank in Zurich," Queally said. "That has been fully checked out by the Department of Finance."

"Who opened the account in Switzerland," Muldowney asked idly. It was an off the cuff question.

Queally put a hand in his pocket and brought out his notebook.

"The arrangements were made by the Bank of England," he answered. "I have the official's name. I was going to ring him later."

"You needn't bother," Muldowney told him. "He won't be there. He's down in the morgue."

Queally was silent. For all his long immersion in the cross referencing payoffs of intelligence gathering he had failed to link the result of a routine inquiry to London with the man who had been found strangled beside the valueless bars of brass. Even when the involvement of a Bank of England official had been disclosed during the interview with Mannheim at the German Embassy, he had stilled failed to join the pieces together. His own trainee had demonstrated far greater perspicacity. It was a singular defeat for a man who prided himself on intellectual superiority.

Muldowney put out his hand for Queally's notebook. The spymaster held on to it but read out a name.

"Charles Edgar."

"Now we can put a name on to the body," Muldowney punished him further.

Queally digested this in further silence.

"Where do we go now," the spymaster asked.

Muldowney directed him back to Finucane's office. He decided that it was time for a major confrontation.

"Follow me," he ordered the compliant head of Section when they had parked. "We're going to get some answers from a member of the government."

Chapter Fourteen

There was no one in Finucane's outer office but even if there had been a civil service guardian in place, Muldowney was in no mood to be stopped. With the spymaster immediately behind him, he strode in on the unsuspecting minister.

Finucane started up from his chair at their entrance. The secretary who had come in from the outer office to take some notes, turned around in alarm. Muldowney ordered the woman out of the room and spoke curtly to the politician. Finucane was looking from Muldowney to Queally and back again. He obviously had not expected to encounter them both together.

"He's got a gun," Queally warned. "Be careful."

The minister sat back in his chair. An armed and dangerous Muldowney was not what he had expected, particularly since a short time before he had seemed to have the agent under control and settled into a quiet corner of the Department.

"There have been some developments," Muldowney snapped out. "We want some answers. The truth this time."

Queally sat down in one of the minister's visitor chairs, seeming totally disoriented by the turn which events had taken. He was a man who operated from a desk. Field work was left to his staff. He perceived his duties as being the receipt and evaluation of information and the preparation of economically phrased reports. He had built his reputation on the ability to sift and manipulate, not through encounters with armed men.

Muldowney had not needed the threat of the imaginary gun in his pocket. He was obviously totally in control. Finucane had all the appearance of a trapped man. The agent's appearance with Queally, the man who in his presence had been ordered to kill the elusive and erratic operative, had for the moment

201

thrown the normally urbane and unshakable politician.

Muldowney addressed the minister.

"You've been hung out to dry," he said. "We want to know where the bullion is.

The Finance minister stared up at his tormentor.

"I don't know," he responded. "I know nothing about it. My instructions from the Committee were to make arrangements for it to go to Zurich through London and Frankfurt. It was an arrangement made through the banks. I know nothing about the people who stole it"

"One way or the other you are going to have to take the blame," Muldowney went on remorselessly. "The Bank of England's man was killed here in Dublin before the bullion left. We know who killed him and we know that it was you who gave the orders."

This last claim was a wild assertion designed to shake up the worried politician even further.

It brought practically no result. The minister was slowly regaining his composure.

"No!" he said forcefully. "The robbery and the murder were nothing to do with me at all. My only involvement was to organize the shipment of the bullion. I'm tired telling you that this was on the Security Committee's orders," he added angrily.

"You'll be charged with murder in due course," Muldowney said, finally satisfied that he was not going to get anything more from the shaken but adamant politician.   In reality he accepted that Finucane knew nothing about the bank official's death, but he was feeling belligerent and Finucane was a convenient victim.

Once again the agent experienced some misgivings about Finucane's role in events. He was certain that he was involved in the robbery of the bullion, but as to the murder of the English bank official, that was something else. Yet the two events had to be connected. If Finucane had not ordered the bank official's killing, then who had.

He turned to Queally.

"Our next stop is the Central Bank. Rodgers has to be a part of this. We'll take Finucane with us."

The Finance minister startcd to protest, growing momentarily angry. Muldowney thrust his hand back into his jacket pocket and pointed his index finger again to simulate his imaginary gun. He swung his hidden hand towards the minister. Finucane got up and walked to the door closely followed by the silent spymaster. Muldowney brought up the rear.

It was initially more difficult to get into Rodgers' headquarters than it had been to gain access to the minister, but as soon as the main door was opened Muldowney pushed the minister and Queally inside and urged them rapidly up the stairs. The doorman brought up the rear, plaintively complaining at this rude and highly irregular invasion, but Muldowney progressed his little party on to Rodgers' office.

It was virtually a rerun of the earlier invasion of Finucane's sanctum. The spymaster again repeated his warning that Muldowney was armed and sank down into one of Rodgers' chairs. They were more ample and luxurious that those provided at public expense in the ministerial chambers. Finucane stood in one corner, wary, expressionless.

203

Muldowney accused the banker of complicity in the plot, of deliberately concealing the existence and identity of the murdered Bank of England official. Rodgers was more alarmed than the minister had been at this accusation, but still Muldowney felt that he was not as heavily involved as the Finance minister.

"I want written statements from both of you," Muldowney said, ordering Finucane to sit at the desk with the banker. "The Director will witness them."

He still felt compelled to address his head of Section as Director even though he knew that this was the man who without compunction had set out to kill him. But the old habits ingrained by years of servility in the minor echelons of the civil service had left their mark. Every superior was due his title and outward respect.

Finucane seemed about to reject the agent's proposal about a statement. Muldowney waved his jacketed fist once more in his direction and he brought out a fountain pen. Rodgers handed him a sheet of paper.

"What do you expect me to put down," Finucane asked.

"State that your organized the shipment of the bullion and sign it," Muldowney ordered.

"That is a matter of record," Finucane said. "The initial Cabinet decision to send the gold to London was processed through my Department. So was the Security Committee order to send it on to Switzerland."

"I want it in my record," Muldowney said shortly. "Write down that you personally gave the orders."

Muldowney felt he knew exactly what he wanted and wasn't

going to be deflected. Whatever the truth eventually proved to be, he was going to have paper to mark every step of the operation. The statements would be added to his file of evidence in safekeeping in his bank. His years in Social Welfare had ingrained in him the necessity of keeping records.

Finucane did as he was told without any further argument. Mukldowney picked up the paper, got Queally to sign as well as a witness and put it in his pocket. He turned his attention to the banker.

"Now you write a statement saying that you allocated the bullion," he said. "Put down every stage of your involvement."

The banker did as he was told and Queally countersigned this statement as well.

When he had finished he reiterated that both men would be arrested and charged in due course. He warned them to do and say nothing that had any bearing on the case.

Finucane spoke up.

"You haven't got anything you know," he said conversationally. "Those statements only establish that we carried out our authorized duties. We had no responsibility for the gold after it left the country."

The banker too was calmer. He had also sized up the situation.

"My function was to get the shipment ready to go to the bank of England,' he said. "My instructions came from the minister's department. I liaised with Mr Edgar on delivery.

He stopped suddenly as the import of what he had just said struck him.

205

"He's dead you say. When?"

"Three days ago," Muldowney responded. "He was strangled."

He gave the banker another piece of paper.

"And now we'll have a statement about your meetings with Edgar," he said quietly, his unhurried tones concealing the jubilation that he felt inside at having tracked this astute and influential man into a further admission simply by pretending that the first simple statement was all that he required.

Now he could prove a link between Rodgers and the murdered Englishman. Queally glanced at him, an expression of reluctant admiration on his face. It was a ploy worthy of the spymaster himself, and one steeped in the devious ethic of the Section.

"I know nothing more about Edgar than I know about the disappearance of the gold," the banker maintained agitatedly. "I am going to make a complaint. This whole line of enquiry is monstrous."

Muldowney nodded his agreement.

"It is indeed," he said. "and you don't known the half of it," he added, catching sight of the spymaster's still worried and perspiring countenance. The prospect of another complaint to higher authority was not something that Queally could handle with equanimity.

"Why was Edgar killed," the banker asked.

Muldowney thought for a moment.

"He was killed because he was doing his job," he answered.

"Someone was trying to cover the route of the gold. He was the link man between the banks. If he was silenced the trail was concealed."

The agent was frustrated at the results of his interrogation. It now seemed as if the banker Rodgers too knew nothing about the death of his English colleague, even though he had not revealed that he was in Dublin when Muldowney had called for the first interview.

The minister spoke this time.

"I think you're right," he said. "But we didn't kill him."

"Then who did," Muldowney demanded.

There was silence in the room. Muldowney turned to the spymaster.

"Cronin killed him," he said. "You gave the orders. You are in this with these two."

He made a gesture with his pointed pocketed finger.

Queally blanched.

"You had Edgar killed," Muldowney repeated. "Cronin carried out that murder. That's why you tried to kill him in the car with me."

He jerked his pocket with its pointed finger at the spymaster once more.

"Now its your turn," he ordered. "I want a statement about the Edgar murder."

Queally shook his head.

207

"You won't get that from me," he said. "I know nothing about it. If Cronin is caught you can hear what he has to say."

The sudden defiance from the seated head of Section surprised the agent for a moment. Could it be that Queally had not in fact ordered the killing of the English banker. He decided to press on.

"Very well," he said. "Now I want to know where the gold is at this point in time."

The three men glanced at each other and there was a long silence. Muldowney realized it seemed that they didn't know. He sat down, suddenly drained. His whole headlong flush of deduction had come to a halt. He had believed that all these men had been involved in the plot at various levels. The Finance minister as the instigator grasping at the opportunities provided by the secrecy surrounding the shipment. The banker as the consignor who had access to all the details, and Queally as the security agent charged with covering up the trail. Suddenly, unexpectedly, the whole thing had come to a dead end once more. The gold had vanished and none of them knew what had happened to it.

"Are you positive that the bullion didn't get to Switzerland," he asked the banker.

"It might be in Switzerland for all we known," Rodgers said. "But it didn't get to the bank we consigned it to and the Swiss would known if it crossed the border."

There was another long silence.

"Who else knows about shipping out the gold," Muldowney asked.

"I told you before, the Cabinet authorized the transfer," the

208

minister grated. "We were only following our instructions. The authorization for the redirection came from the Security Committee."

"Can you prove this," Muldowney demanded.

The original decision would have been minuted by the Cabinet secretary," Finucane said. "I gave the order to my Department head when I went back to the office. After that it as all paper work."

"It wasn't all paper work," Muldowney responded. "A man was strangled."

He rounded on Queally. The luckless spymaster drew away from him. Muldowney limited his aggression to posturing anger and fired another sharp question at him.

"Who gave you your orders?"

Minister and banker looked at the spymaster. They were glances that spelled surprise and Muldowney realised that they had no knowledge of any role by Queally in the affair.

"He takes his orders directly from the Security Committee," Finucane said. "Whatever he did, he did on their instructions."

Queally licked his bloodless lips and toom off his spectacles to wipe the lenses. He put them back on and faced his accuser.

"My orders are secret," he said. "You know that. And you forget something," he looked sharply at Muldowney, "you work for me. You take orders from me. I ask the questions."

"You tried to kill me," Muldowney rejoined. "I'm giving the orders now."

Muldowney was lost in his thoughts for a moment or two. He turned to Queally again. He grasped the import of what Finucane had said. If Queally wasn't operating for minister and banker, then he was working for someone else. The logic of the situation dictated that if Queally had ordered the killing of the English banker then he had done so at the behest of people who outranked both. Finucane and the deputy governor of the bank. This could only be the Security Committee.

A thought stuck him.

"Why did you send me out on this mission," he asked the spymaster.

Queally was silent for a moment or two.

"I didn't," he said. "You got into this yourself. I was running you blind. I wanted to raise some work files, nothing more."

Muldowney considered this response for a moment or two. It rang true. Queally had been covering up for lack of work. He realized that the spymaster had done nothing at all to steer him towards the conspiracy. Muldowney's entire linkup with it had been an accidental encounter with a girl in a pub which Queally had no part in at all. If O'Connor hadn't got drunk and looked for some dangerous female diversion that night, he would known nothing, Muldowney thought a trifle bitterly. The exhilaration of the chase had worn off somewhat. He realized that his situation was still highly precarious even though he had come a fair distance along the trail. He had got his hands on two conspirators and his own murderous boss. Yet he was still a long way off being able to furnish positive proof of anything to the Security Committee.

He considered Finucane's position for a moment. There had been guilt there all along. Right from the beginning, Muldowney had detected an uneasiness in the minister which

210

signified some sort of wrong doing. Then it struck Muldowney. Finucane had been double dealing. He had seen an opportunity to skim off the top. He thought for a moment. There would be valuation charges and commissions due as the gold moved through the various currency systems. He and Rodgers were putting these commissions in their pockets. They might have even intended to keep some of the bullion for themselves. That was one angle. But the agent was still convinced that Finucane played a bigger role. He knew where the gold was, Muldowney was certain.

But this line of thought brought him no further forward. The bullion was still missing. Who had it and how did they get it. He turned to Queally.

"If they didn't steal the bullion who did?"

"No one knew about the shipment outside the Cabinet, the Security Committee and the bank," Finucane said.

He also looked at Queally.

That was probably true Muldowney decided. That meant that an arm of government had a part in the affair. He wondered again about the dead bank official, Edgar. He had been killed because he was the hands on link between the different banks. Had he also diverted the final transfer away from the Zurich bank to some other venue. Was his work finished when he had rerouted the gold. Had he been killed because he knew too much.

Who had killed him? The facts such as they were pointed to Cronin, acting on Queally's orders. Queally was either in the plot or he had got direct instructions from the Security Committee. A new twist to the matter entered Muldowney's mind. Supposing it was the Security Committee itself which was running the operation. Supposing they had taken control of the situation to protect themselves. This theory began to make some sense. It could explain a great deal.

The more he thought about it, the more Muldowney believed that he had hit on the truth. All the people that he had got to so far, Rodgers, the murdered banker Edgar, and the dead alcoholic officer, O'Connor, were cogs in the machine, carrying out orders while not really knowing much about the overall planning. He had little doubt now that he was on the right track. Finucane and Mannheim on the other hand were definitely key figures. The role of the Security Committee was not yet clearly defined. Queally definitely worked for the Committee.

The banker was the first to speak. He had been silent for most of the time.

"I think we should call in the police," he said.

He looked askance at Queally.

"I don't want to have anything to do with your department."

Queally stood up. He had composed himself now and was once again as quiet and stealthy as the spider he resembled. Muldowney perceived with some alarm that the spymaster was taking over again. He moved his muffled gun hand once more but Queally ignored it.

"We outrank the police," Queally told the banker. "We control all the services. This is a matter for my department and no other."

"But one of your people has killed a man," the banker protested. "Your own agent admitted it."

Queally ignored the outburst. He went to the telephone and made a call, cupping his hand around the mouthpiece to prevent them from hearing what was being said.

After that he addressed Muldowney "We have an appointment," he said. "You are to come as well," he said to the minister. "There is no need for us to intrude on you any longer, Mr Rodgers. Just keep yourself available in case we have to make further enquiries."

He nodded knowingly to the banker who blanched and fell back into his chair. It was clear that he definitely had fears about clandestine arrangements coming into the light of day.

They got into Queally's car and the spymaster drove quickly through the terraced and long defoliated College Green and up Dawson street to the still lush acres of St Stephens Green which Lord Ardilaun had given to the citizens. Muldowney had often walked its flower trimmed paths and thrown bits of bread to the ducks, but these pleasant pursuits were far from his mind as the spymaster pulled up outside the mansion which housed the Department of External Affairs.

Iveagh House too had been a Guinness family gift. They went inside and Queally led them up an imposing staircase to the first floor. Muldowney had put in many hours in government offices but this building was a different experience altogether. Sumptuously carpeted and furnished it seemed more like a luxury hotel than a department of state. The few people they met in the corridors went about their business in a silent hushed differential manner as if overcome by the dignity of their surroundings. Here, he realized, was a citadel of real power. This was the Security Committee chairman's own department.

The spymaster knocked on a door and led them into the room. They sat across the table from the Grim Grey Men. There were five of them, the full Security Committee in session. When he realized where he was, Finucane went to walk around to the ministers' side of the table, but the Chairman was having none of it. He pointed silently to a chair beside the spymaster. Just as silently Finucane sat down.

Queally was nervous. Finucane no less so, although he was more often in the company of ministerial colleagues. However, these were a select band of ministers, all powerful men who it seemed had the power of life and death, and judging by events were not adverse to using it. Finucane himself had been present when they had given the spymaster instructions to eliminate his own innocent agent. Did they know, Finucane wondered, if the target of that death sentence was now in the room with them.

Queally made his report in the form of short verbal paragraphs. He had interviewed the German diplomat, the Finance minister who had come with them, and the deputy governor of he Central Bank. He had also brought with him agent Muldowney, he said, and stopped significantly for a second or two. One or two of the Grim Grey Men shifted uncomfortably, but the Chairman looked coldly and dispassionately at the secret agent across the table.

"You have caused us a great deal of trouble, Mr Muldowney," he said.

Muldowney felt intimidated, but decided that he wasn't going to be domineered by these people.

"I am a very troublesome person," he said with forced flippancy.

The time had come, he decided, for him to upstage Queally and make an impression upon these men who ruled with such ruthless decision.

THE IRISH SECRET AGENT

"You have killed two people, and probably a third person," the Chairman remarked casually.

Muldowney looked at the men across from him. They were all stern, grey, grizzled elders, no strangers to violence in their day, he thought, but now all of them were upholders of the world of democracy. Into their new world of administration and government there now rarely strayed any taste of what once had been their ordinary ways of dealing with events. Yet that they could order the deaths of people without compunction and in defiance of legal authority, showed quite clearly how little they feared the force of law or indeed any moral imperative.

Muldowney decided to fight back.

"Two men died in accidents in circumstances which arose in the course of my investigations. The post mortems will prove that."

"A post mortem will prove what we want it to prove," the Chairman said curtly. He didn't like being argued with.

"The third man, the English banker was killed on your instructions," Muldowney countered. "And after that you ordered me to be killed as well."

The silence in the room was loaded with menace. The leader of the Grim Grey Men, however, was only disconcerted for a moment.

"You have been running around the city like a lunatic," the Chairman said.

"What else did you expect me to do. I am a sworn official of the state," Muldowney rejoined, "charged with upholding law and order. I expect to be protected by the government which I

215

am trying to serve."

"We will decide who will be protected," the Chairman answered.

One of the others spoke up.

"You're a very unusual man," he said. "Not at all what we expected."

"I'm a secret agent," Muldowney responded. "I'm not supposed to be what you expect."

"And a very good one too, obviously," one of the others remarked. "You seem to have got right into the middle of this matter despite the efforts of your superior to prevent you from doing so."

He gave a quick glance at the spymaster, as his remarks brought a low short cut laugh around the table.

Queally winced at the jibe but made no response.

"So where are you now in your investigations," the Chairman asked.

Muldowney put his hands on the table.

"We've come to a dead end," he said. "We have a complete paper trail. I have copies of all the documents in a safe place, and I have statements from Minister Finucane and the banker, Rodgers, to confirm the arrangements."

"Documents," the Chairman repeated.

"That's right,' Muldowney said. "The file of papers was being passed on to the minister here."

216

He indicated Finucane.

"But I intercepted them and got copies made. They are in a safe place," he added. "A very safe place."

"I have copies as well," Queally put in.

He gave no further information but the implications were obvious. The two security agents, chief and operative, were each protecting themselves by retaining replicas of the paper trail which tracked the bullion out of the country.

The Chairman considered for a moment.

"These documents merely show the authorized arrangements made to move the bullion," he said. "I don't see why you consider such records so important."

"They will reveal if these transactions were in fact carried out on behalf of the state," Muldowney said. "They also carry the signatures of the officials who were involved along the way. I believe that in fact the transfer of the gold beyond London was not authorized by the government. This Committee decided to move it for reasons of its own. Then the gold was stolen and now the Committee is in trouble. The decision to move it to Switzerland was outside your authority. The English bank official was killed to prevent any of this information getting out."

Queally spoke up.

"I have a copy of the original Cabinet minute," he said. "It is very specific. The gold was to go to the Bank of England and nowhere else. There is no record of any other decision being taken by the government."

Everyone was silent. Muldowney gave Queally full credit for

his bombshell. He had put his finger right on the spot. The Cabinet had authorized the transfer of the bullion to England, but the men in this room had ordered it to be moved on further. If they couldn't recover the bullion they were in serious trouble.

The Grim Grey Men considered in silence for several minutes. The Chairman held a whispered conversation with one of them and then spoke to Muldowney.

"What are your conclusions," he asked.

Muldowney decided to take the plunge. He had nothing to lose at this stage. They had already tried to kill him and might indeed try again. But he knew that he had frightened them with the fact that he held copies of the shipment papers. These led all the way to Zurich, but somewhere along the way the gold had disappeared.

"I am certain that this Committee changed the government's orders and acted unlawfully, possibly for good reasons. You people have sufficient power to carry through your own decisions. No one would question you. Finucane was instructed to initiate the procedures. Rodgers in the Central Bank was to liaise with the other banks. Then I made my report and you learned that there was a plot to double cross you and steal the gold. Mr Queally was instructed to investigate the situation and trap the conspirators."

He paused for a moment to wet his lips. He could have done with a glass of water but there was none on the table.

"You shouldn't have brought in Queally," he told them. "He runs a make believe service. He isn't an intelligence agent, he's a bluffer, a yarn spinner, and I think he's probably mad. But you needed him. You are in trouble over the gold and if it becomes public you will all be disgraced."

218

"Cronin killed the Englishman," he went on. "He made the mistake of leaving the body where he dumped the brass. I don't know who gave him his orders, but he should not have allowed anything to link the dead man with our Section. It was bad work."

He thought for a few moments.

"You went after me because I was causing too many problems. I was loose and causing headlines. I had to be stopped."

The leader of the Grim Grey Men folded his hands in front of him.

"We regret that you should have been a target for perhaps what was a mistaken decision by this Committee," he said smoothly. "However, that is behind us. We now have a situation which calls for further action."

Muldowney looked him straight in the face.

"The only action that is required," he said bravely, "is that you should bring back the gold and replace it in the state bank."

"We might perhaps agree with you about that," the other replied. "However, there is a problem. We don't know where the gold is either. It has disappeared completely."

Muldowney stared at him.

"You don't know where it is" he echoed.

The other opened his hands in a gesture of baffled ignorance.

"That is the situation," he said. "We ourselves are now in a very difficult position. We moved the gold on from London for a particular purpose. We have been duped. The plotters succeeded. We have to find out who has stolen the bullion from us and get it back."

The Chairman spoke directly to Finucane for the first time.

"Have you any ideas about this, Malachy," he asked.

The Finance minister shook his head. It appeared that he was as astonished as Muldowney.

"We have to come to terms with you," the grey leader said to Muldowney. "You have the whip hand. We understand that. Your life is obviously safe because of the fact that you have the documents. In any event we are not interested in pursuing you. We cannot afford any further complications. The police will be called off. And, of course, others."

He looked meaningfully at the spymaster.

"What we want you to do is to find out what happened to the gold," he went on. "In the meantime nothing will happen to you and we will eventually put this whole matter behind us. You will report to Queally. He will as usual be the channel between your department and ourselves."

He thought for a moment.

"We do not have to explain our motives to you," he said finally, "but I feel that I should say to you on behalf of this Committee, that our decision to move this gold was taken for the good of the country and for no other reason."

He extended a cold white hand across the table to the secret agent. Muldowney took it for a moment and let go.

THE IRISH SECRET AGENT

"It has been an experience to meet you, Mr Muldowney," the Chairman said. "My colleague is quite right. You are a most unusual man."

Chapter Fifteen

Muldowney left Queally outside the External Affairs building, telling the spymaster that he had enquiries to make and would check in later. He walked across St Stephen's Green and came out at the corner beside the Shelbourne Hotel. He had nowhere in particular to go. It was late afternoon and the city was busy with hurrying shoppers. Acting on an impulse he walked on down to Merrion Square, passing the wrought iron railings guarding the buildings at the rear of the parliament building Leinster House and turned into the gateway that gave access to the National Gallery.

He had never been inside before and the graceful solitude of the great portraits hanging in the ante rooms found a sympathetic response in his own feeling of loneliness. He shook off his depression and concentrated on the reason for his visit. Somewhere in the vastness of the galleries he expected to find Joyce Dolan. This was her world, the focus of what she was about and he entered it diffidently.

He didn't ask for her at the porter's desk but kept moving more or less aimlessly from one vast silent room to another, glancing casually from time to time at the nation's pictorial treasures in their elaborate almost gothic style gilded frames.

He half expected to find her standing lost in rapt worship before one of the masterpieces, perhaps dressed in a smock and carrying a renovating paintbrush and a smeared palette. It was something of a minor shock when he caught sight of her sitting on one of the benches which the gallery provided for fatigued and perhaps less dedicated viewers.

But it was not the sight of Joyce Dolan that made him slip into the concealment of a convenient doorway. It was her companion, the German diplomat Mannheim. They were sitting alone in a long room, half turned to each other and talking animatedly. There was an air of intimacy about them

222

which was reinforced by the fact that they were holding hands. It was not, Muldowney decided, a clasping of totally committed affection. The German was providing reassurance and support with the gesture.

Muldowney watched them for a moment or two. Their intense conversation continued. Once or twice the diplomat patted the woman's shoulder reassuringly. Whatever was being discussed was serious, that was obvious. Muldowney frowned, trying to put this new and unexpected development in perspective. The German had been at the reception in Dublin Castle, conceivably he and Joyce knew each other if they went on the same social round. At the same moment, Muldowney recollected that it had been Finucane that he had seen talking to the German.

Now Joyce Dolan and the diplomat were here together involved in what was obviously a far from casual conversation. On the face of things there was nothing unusual in their being seen together. The agent already knew that the German had official dealings with Finucane so there was no real reason why he should not have social contacts with the minister's mistress. But Muldowney knew instinctively that there was more to it than that. The body language of the couple displayed a much closer bonding that that of friends of a friend. They had met in this quiet empty place by arrangement and that arrangement hallmarked a much deeper relationship.

Muldowney backed off and made his way quickly out of the gallery. He found a taxi as rapidly as possible and sent it towards Joyce Dolan's Rathgar home. He made his way through his own access point from the back garden and once inside began a systematic search of every cupboard, drawer and container that he could find. It was in her dressing table drawers of his own room that he finally found evidence that persuaded him even further that he was on the right track.

223

There was a programme from a concert staged by the German Cultural Institute and an old invitation to a cocktail party in the German Embassy. Then tucked away in a folder he turned out up to a dozen handwritten letters. They were in German, and Muldowney was unable to decipher what they said, but it was evident from their opening and closing greetings that they were love letters, addressed to Joyce and signed Arnold.

The letters were written on private stationery embossed with a crest. Muldowney grimaced in satisfaction. The effacing Herr Mannheim was indeed more than he seemed. He had no doubt, even though he had never seen such a thing before, that the crest on the notepaper was that of an old German military family. Probably a Prussian, he thought, for no better reason that it was images of stern, stiffbacked scions of that militaristic tradition that came to mind, but in fact he was partly wrong. The diplomat was indeed using his family's crest on his notepaper, but he was a Bavarian, with the subtle implications for the business in hand that such origins implied.

Muldowney sat down on the bed and absently fingered the sheets of notepaper. They confirmed the relationship which he had begun to suspect following the chance encounter in the picture gallery. But what did it mean. It seemed that Finucane was being cuckolded, and yet Joyce Dolan seemed too nice a person to be doing it deliberately. He had some inkling of what the scene might have been, the widow lonely after the death of her husband, meeting up with a powerful attractive man, either diplomat or minister, perhaps both around the same time. She falls more under the spell of the German, who persuades her into a relationship which undermines the one which she had established with Finucane.

And yet Muldowney was fairly certain that she liked the politician. There was a softness in her way of dealing with him, but perhaps it was the very nature of his ambition that had sent her towards the German. It was obvious that

224

Finucane, deeply centred on the pursuit of power and under vastly more pressure than would be put upon a diplomat had very little time to spare from his workload for the woman who was being challenged for his affections.

The agent wondered which of the two was the more genuine. He had not spent sufficient time with the German to really decide but instinctively he felt that the diplomat had the edge on the Irish politician. They would undoubtedly both be ruthless but in different ways. The German motivated perhaps by loftier ideals of duty and family. The politician by a strong desire for power, but fuelled more directly by greed and the hidden inherent sense of inferiority which lurked behind so many iof the men who practiced his trade.

The front door opened and he heard the woman's heels on the polished wooden floor of the hall. He put the letters back in their hiding place and lay down on the bed pretending to be asleep as he heard her coming up the stirs. She paused for a moment outside his door, looked in and seemed relieved to find him there. She was pleased to see him in her home rather than out on the trail in pursuit of whatever new revelation lay in store, Muldowney decided.

He went downstairs and Joyce poured them both a drink. He sipped reflectively wondering how to start the inquisition that he must inevitably get into. She was quiet as well, sensing that Muldowney had something serious coming up.

He decided to get an insight into her association with the National Gallery. She worked there part time and was also chairperson of a fund raising committee, she told him. There was a constant need for money, not just to buy important paintings when they came on the market but to maintain the collection. They had display and storage problems. Indeed the space available was far too little to properly present the many hundreds of pictures the State in fact possessed,   most of them she admitted, inherited from the colonial past. The new rulers of Ireland, although numbering some cultured figures in their ranks, had little time and less money to devote to what the vast majority of the populace would have considered a vaguely worthy but supremely dilettentist cause.

She spoke animatedly, warming to an obviously well cherished theme of enthusiasm for her task yet coloured with a slight but unmistakable bitterness at the difficulties which faced those who would attempt to instill some semblance of culture amongst an unresponsive citizenry. For the most part they were far too concerned with earning a living in times which for many, did not seem to have improved from the hungry thirties and forties.

Muldowney knew little about art of any kind. The worlds of paintings, sculpture and literature were not so much alien to him as realms which could not be penetrated because there was never the time to do so. There were other restraints. Culture was ring fenced by many puritanical conventions. Even many of the great presentations of the cinema were denied to Irish audiences because of the pervasive influence of bullying overseers of moral rectitude. Muldowney also was well aware that the written word too offered countless opportunities for perceived depravity and the subversion of public morals. Indeed as part of his duties in Queally's office he had from time to time been required to visit booksellers and prepare reports of the existence of certain works for forwarding to the Censors office.

It was perhaps surprising that he had not been sent to the gallery in the line of duty for there were certainly on public exhibition some works which by their exposure of naked flesh must have posed some threat of moral disintegration so feared by the righteous guardians of public morality.

But this proximity to such enthusiasm for art and pictures was something new to him. Even his visit to the gallery earlier in the afternoon had been totally overlaid by his quest for the woman who now sat talking so animatedly to him in her own home. He had seen the great pictures hanging so majestically in their places but they had meant nothing to him. Indeed it was more than obvious that they meant nothing to the vast majority of the population, for the gallery had contained only a handful of people and nearly all of these had been visitors from other countries.

Muldowney waited for an opportunity to steer the conversation towards the real subject of his probe, her relationship with the German diplomat Mannheim. His opportunity came when she started to compare the sparse Irish public purse with the policies pursued in other countries.

"The war must have destroyed a great many treasures," he remarked, trying to interject a new dimension into the conversation.

"Europe is full of looted art treasures," she said. "The Nazis collected the best works from all the countries they invaded and took them back to Germany by the train load. Many of them have been lost, but they are being recovered slowly but surely," she said.

"Have you been to Germany," Muldowney asked.

She nodded.

"I've been to Munich a few times," she said. "It's a wonderful city. Very much like Dublin. In fact," she added reflectively, "the people are very similar to the Irish. I would have spent more time in Germany but for the war," she went on. "My parents often went to Stuttgart and to Berlin. My other had relations, distant cousins, I think, in both cities."

She looked at him keenly.

"Are you interested in Germany," she asked. "It's a very fine country, the people are very self reliant and very determined too. They will become prosperous again, except for the east, of course. The Russians will have to go before there is much improvement there."

The conversation was digressing and Muldowney decided to bring it back on track.

"I know an official in the German Embassy," he said. "He's the trade attaché, Mannheim."

A small bit of colour came into her cheeks but otherwise there was no sign of discomposure. Muldowney chose his words carefully.

"I think you have a more personal relationship with Germany than through your parents," he said.

Another tinge of colour came to her cheeks. He looked at her with a hint of sternness in both his voice and face.

"What do you mean" she countered.

"You are directly connected to two major figures in my investigation," he said slowly. "I would describe you in fact as a woman in the middle. I think you are an important link in the plan."

He stopped for a moment and looked her straight in the face. She met his glance for a second then turned away to find her cigarettes. She lit up with a slight tremor in her hands and waited for Muldowney to speak again.

"I want to know the situation," he said. "Are you working with Mannheim or are you working with Finucane. Your personal relationship with either man is of no interest to me."

This time she blushed outright. He decided to run one of the bluffing ploys so favoured by the detective O'Brien. It was the inquisitorial weapon of portraying total knowledge which had led to the unraveling of the first few threads of them web of deceit which cloaked the theft of the gold.

"I know all about you," he said. "I know where your loyalties lie, and I know that these are not with Finucane."

It was a gamble but one which was hugely successful.

She blew out a small stream of smoke and sighed in submission.

"I liked Malachy a lot until I met up with Arnhold," she said. "Malachy, I suppose filled a void after my husband's death, but he is a flawed man. I only found that out lately," she added, her mouth tensing slightly in an uncontrollable motion of disdain.

"Which of them has stolen the gold," Muldowney asked.

She was silent for a moment or to.

"Malachy came up with the original idea," she said. "But he got greedy and began to look for a payoff for himself. He was going to keep some of the gold. That man Rodgers was brought into it on that basis as well."

Muldowney nodded. That Rodgers was tied up in it in some way was part of his own thinking. It was inevitable that even the most worthy of causes would have to employ people who would serve only for a fee. Therefore the concept of a corrupt banker did not surprise him. Under the counter payments were not a novelty in the banker's trade.

"Give me the background to it all," he said quietly, anxious not to disturb her willingness to reveal things with any possibility of disconcerting her with threats.

Arnhold has important pictures to sell," she said. "They are from collections seized by the German authorities during the war. He was an officer in command of one of the detachments moving the pictures when the Allies invaded Germany. He hid them and escaped. The money isn't for himself," she added quickly, anxious to justify the diplomat's position. "The proceeds will got to help his colleagues get a new start. There are many officers whose lives have been devastated by the changes in both parts of Germany. They could not go on with their military careers. Treasures like these are being sold around the world to fund them. We can get some of them for Ireland."

"These pictures are stolen from their owners," Muldowney countered.

She shrugged.

"The big national collections have been returned," she said. "Many of the owners of the smaller collections are dead. They have no relatives left. This way some good can come from it. We will get some fantastic pictures. The German officers will get money to start a new life."

Muldowney was silent for a few moments. It was a disturbing tale but it explained many things.

"Why did you have to steal gold to finance this deal," he asked. "Why not organize the money legitimately. It would have been less complicated."

"Malachy said the state couldn't buy looted pictures," she explained. "Then he came up with the idea about the gold. I went in because the country was getting priceless treasures in return for the state's money. We had to take the gold. Malachy said there was no way that we could actually divert any cash from a government account to pay for the pictures," she went on. "A million pounds in money could be traced in banks as it was changed into different currencies. We would never get away with it. Gold can be sold anywhere in the world, in any quantity, if you know how to do it. This was what the Germans wanted. It was their only viable alternative to using European currencies. They couldn't raise enough German money to buy dollars."

Muldowney was fascinated, not just with the woman's tale but with the matter of fact manner in which she told it.

"Surely it was much more risky to try and steal a million pounds in bullion," he asked.

"Not at all," was her response. "In fact there was less possibility of there being any trouble."

Muldowney was inclined to agree. He was certain that the government would be so embarrassed at losing the gold that nothing would ever get out to the public. Once it was realized that the bullion had gone missing in Europe, the investigation would be dropped.

"Tell me more about the German end of it," he commanded.

"The German officers have an organization which helps them," she said. "There are many influential people who support it. Many of them are leading financiers and bankers. The Irish don't have a lot of weight in international financial circles. It was easy to put the government under pressure and get a decision to move the gold to support the currency. It was to go to London officially but arrangements were made with the bank of England to move it on to Germany and then to a bank in Switzerland."

"It didn't get to Switzerland," Muldowney said. "What happened to it?"

"The Germans looked after that end of it," she said. "It was a very skilful operation," she commented. "The Irish authorities were under the impression that they were making a payoff to financial speculators through the Swiss bank. But this was a ruse to conceal the real recipients. The German officers simply picked up the gold at Frankfurt with their own set of documents and took it on to Munich."

"They knew that the Irish wouldn't pay up without making some effort to track down the blackmailers. The idea was to make the Irish authorities concentrate on Zurich as the destination of the gold so that any investigation that they might put on would focus on Switzerland. The authorities would be going after international financial fraudsters who didn't exist. The involvement of the German officers network wouldn't come out at all."

Muldowney had to concede that it was a very shrewd scheme indeed.

"Our country isn't at any loss," she assured him earnestly. "The pressure on our currency will be lifted. The paintings will eventually be much more valuable than the bullion. No one was actually stealing anything."

Muldowney considered the whole thing in silence for a while.

"How did you plan the sudden appearance of these pictures,"

he asked. "Somebody is bound to ask questions."

"That is where Malachy comes in," "He is to present them to the National Gallery as an anonymous donation made through his Department. Once they are in the country they would be secure. The original owners would never be traced. We would have some beautiful things for the gallery. Even if there were any living claimants it would be most unlikely that they would ever come here."

"So the whole thing has been done in the name of irish culture," Muldowney said.

She nodded.

"No one was at any loss," she said. "The paintings belonged to the defeated German army. They had been missing for years and were disposable. We were retrieving them for posterity and in years to come Ireland's reputation would grow. The question of how they came to be here would never arise. The government and the gallery would have a file which said that they were donated by a private benefactor. No one was at any loss," she repeated.

"The difficulty I have with this," Muldowney commented, "is that the Irish government was blackmailed into giving up the gold. The government hasn't agreed to buy these paintings. In fact it doesn't even know they exist."

She nodded agreement.

"I accept that now," she said. "I didn't look at it like that at the beginning. But Malachy soured it for me by looking for personal profit. He was going to keep some of the bullion for himself. That is why Arnhold came up with the plan to cut him out and whip the bullion away in Germany. I thought Malachy was motivated by getting the pictures for the country. I really did."

She was clearly very genuine, Muldowney felt. He was astonished that such a woman would get so far out of her depth and take such great risks for what seemed to him to be a highly ephemeral motive. But there was more to the situation than Finucane's greed and the loss of the woman's belief in the purity of the motives of her former lover.

"A man was killed," Muldowney told her.

He explained the circumstances of the death of the Bank of England official, Edgar. She was obviously shocked.

"Edgar was killed to ensure secrecy," he said. "He was the Bank of England's man on the spot. The Central Bank here told London that the gold was going to Zurich to get the pressure off the Irish currency. The Bank of England collaborated by providing false clearance for the gold to go to its own vaults in London. It was Edgar's job to arrange this piece of camouflage and also to move the bullion on to Switzerland. He arranged for the opening of a numbered account in the Zurich bank believing that it would be drawn down from there as arranged. He had to come to Dublin to check the serial numbers on the ingots."

"Edgar must have got suspicious, perhaps Rodgers gave something away," he went on. "He was loyal to the governments. He might have found out that Finucane and Rodgers were part of the currency pressure conspiracy. Or perhaps he just caught on to Finucane's attempt to take a cut himself. He might have been killed because he had a grip on the whole operation and was dangerous. We shall never know."

Joyce seemed totally stunned.

234

"Killed," she said. "Are you sure?"

"He was strangled," Muldowney said shortly. "I believe that one of my colleagues may have killed him."

She was silent.

Muldowney resumed his rationalization of events.

"I believe that someone in the Security Committee gave the order to have him killed," he said. "They were the only ones who could have given that kind of order, whether directly to my colleague or through the system. I think they had to protect themselves."

She was genuinely shocked at what he had said. He could see that. They were silent for another while.

Another point struck the secret agent.

"The officers have the gold in their possession," he said, "but how are the pictures to get here?"

"The German Cultural Institute is having an exhibition of German art in a couple of weeks time," she said. "The pictures will come in as part of that shipment, but won't be put on display. They will be sent to the Gallery. I will catalogue them and put them into store until an opportunity comes up to exhibit them. They won't all be left in the Gallery," she said. "Some of them will go to the President's house, others will be hung in government departments and so on."

Muldowney sat back in his chair overcome by the turn which her narrative had taken. That it was all true he had no doubt. All the pieces had now fallen into place. Everyone so far identified with the affair had his particular individual part to play. The German diplomat had sold the idea to the Irish

Finance minister. The officer network had used its connections to put pressure on the Irish currency. The government responded by deciding to support the Irish pound by increasing its gold reserves with the Bank of England.

The Security Committee had been given the task of transferring the bullion to London and put Finucane in charge of what at that stage was believed to be a straightforward response to normal financial pressures. Rodgers had set the banking wheels in motion. Then the Committee discovered that the campaign against the currency was organized. It decided to use the bullion as bait, hoping that they would catch the blackmailers.

They had lost the gold and Edgar was murdered, not because he had anything to do with the crime, but because he could reveal that the Security Committee had been outwitted and the bullion was gone. Five high ranking careers were on the line. Their reputations and political future were more important to the Grim Grey Men that Edgar's life.

That Joyce had gone along with the scheme from the purest of motives, Muldowney had no doubt. She would have had no knowledge that a man would be killed to ensure secrecy. It had taken her some time as well to realize that Finucane and the banker, Rodgers, had dirtied their bibs to make a sideline profit.

Muldowney's contempt for Finucane grew. He had been ouwitted by his mistress and the German diplomat and now was on the brink of being exposed. It was clear from the curt manner in which the Security Committee had dealt with Finucane that morning that they themselves suspected him of something. They would know their man and would deal with him, although they would have to be circumspect. Finucane, like Edgar, could disclose that the Committee had been blackmailed, had sent the bullion on from London and had lost

236

it. It was unlikely, however that Finucane would be killed.

Whatever happened, Muldowney felt sure the story would never get into the public domain. Finucane would be dismissed on some pretext, but he would be safe from any serious penalty. Unless, of course, they decided to keep the whole situation really clean and arrange an accident. The Security Committee had a lot at stake. They had made a grevious mistake by deciding to see off the currency threat without taking the full government into their confidence. Their actions were unauthorized and illegal. They would be held accountable for the loss of the gold. Their careers would be destroyed.

Muldowney's immediate problem now was to decide what he should do. The Security Committee had taken him off the wanted list but there was still a major crime to be solved. Muldowney was responsible for his own unfortunate encounters with the soldier and the photographer which had led to their deaths, but the question of the strangled bank official was another matter altogether. It was highly unlikely that the banker's identity could remain suppressed for long. The murdered man provided a story which the English papers seemed very likely to pick up, and there could well be questions in the British and Irish parliaments.

Someone would have to pay for that murder, Muldowney felt sure. The most likely candidate seemed to be Cronin who had probably carried it out. Muldowney wasn't sure whether he wanted to go after his colleague personally or not. It seemed that the best approach would be to let matters take their course. If the pressure came on then the police would pursue his fellow agent. The important thing for Muldowney was to make sure that he held enough cards to prevent anyone going after himself.

There were more immediate and important considerations than

Cronin and the dead bank official. Muldowney was certain now that he had uncovered the major details of the plot. The question was what was he to do. The bullion was gone. The chances of getting it back remote. There were obvious difficulties involved in getting the Security Committee to authorize contact with the German authorities. A hunt for missing gold held by former Nazi officers would be seriously undermined by the fact that the search would have to be made in Bavaria, home of the Nazi movement

Local agencies there would have to be brought in, and it seemed highly likely that the Bavarian police and other state bodies would not be too exacting in their efforts to comply with a hunt for vanished Irish gold. Apart from the logistics of the situation, the bureaucratic complexities would be enormous.

The best approach would be to concentrate on ensuring the safe delivery of the pictures to Ireland. At least that would ensure that the Irish authorities held a consideration for the gold that they had so naively released.

How could he be certain that the pictures would arrive with the exhibition. He voiced his concerns.

"They'll arrive alright,' she said. "I have no doubts whatsoever. I wouldn't be a party to the scheme if I thought it wasn't going to benefit the country. Ireland will get its money's worth and the pictures will hang here in Dublin."

"But the gold has gone," he argued. "There is no way of enforcing the German end of the contract."

She smiled at him, amused for a moment by his concerns. But underneath her assurance about the arrival of the paintings there were other worries. He had totally unnerved her with his disclosure about the killing of the English bank official.

"I've already been to Munich to select and value the paintings," she said. "Malachy insisted on that. He said we had to ensure that we were getting value for money."

Muldowney marveled for a moment at the scruples of the minister who was prepared to line his own pockets with a cut from the unlawful disposal of his country's gold to privateering foreign officers and yet at the same time wanted to make sure that his country got a fair balance of value in return for its money.

Muldowney now had other worries. He began to wonder how much of this he should report to Queally. There was no real proof of anything. All that he had in terms of documentary evidence was the various signatures on the different memoranda and consignment notes lodged in his bank for safe keeping. But the importance of these items had been overtaken by events. They were good as far as they went. The paper trail and the people who had authorized the various stages could be identified, but nothing more. It was clear, of course, that the Security Committee had taken it on themselves to reroute the gold to Germany and then to the bank in Switzerland. He had no proof that the Nazis had stolen it, any more than he could prove that the Grim Grey Men had ordered the killing of the bank official.

If he reported Joyce Dolan and Mannheim as conspirators and they were arrested, the pictures might never get to Dublin. The German could not be charged with any offence, but the very fact of his exposure would make the dispatch of the paintings to Ireland highly improbable. The officer network with its haul of bullion in hand as well as the paintings would just disappear.

Muldowney made up his mind. He would have to go along with the situation. The gold was gone and the politicians would have to deal with that loss as best they could. The

239

nation would get the paintings which according to Joyce were equivalent in value. The woman had resolved the moral dilemma as far as she was concerned with this switch. The principle was just as valid for Muldowney. He had no interest in the rights of any original owners of the pictures. After all, the fruits of piracy had built many great empires, personal and public, and it was in the nature of things that some people should suffer and others prosper from such happenings.

Of course, the nation would never know that it had profited from the transaction. Indeed it would probably never learn that it had lost a million pounds in gold. The Grim Grey Men would never let such information out. They could never allow it to be known that they had been swindled. They had already killed a man to protect themselves. Since the public knew little about bullion held in the vaults of the Central Bank, it would not be greatly perplexed one way or another.

However, Muldowney had his career and personal safety to consider. He could not let any private disposition towards accepting Joyce Dolan's appreciation of art to put him in any kind of jeopardy. He made up his mind. He needed to get across to the Security Committee that he was on top of the situation. Queally would have to be told to set up a meeting.

He telephoned the spymaster's office. Queally was as usual in his lair. Muldowney speculated briefly as to what other clandestine affairs occupied him in his continuous sojourn high above the city. Queally often liked to joke that when he looked out of is window over O'Connell street he could see that only Nelson on his column stood between himself and God. Muldowney often thought that the spymaster believed that he himself was God and if that was the case, then surely recent events had somewhat dented his personal image.

"I need to meet the Security Committee," the secret agent said. "As soon as possible."

His tone was peremptory. Queally reacted with an angry refusal. It was not possible. Muldowney was forgetting himself. The Chairman had made it quite clear. The agent was to report through his superior. The chain of command was not going to be bypassed.

"This information must be given to them direct," Muldowney responded shortly. "We can both go if you wish. Otherwise I will make my own arrangements."

Queally was silent for a moment. He was surprised at the vehemence in Muldowney's tones although he had realized from their last encounter that his once compliant and naïve subordinate had very rapidly become a tough, steely and formidable operative.

"I'll see what I can do," the spymaster finally acquiesced.

He went on to another phone line. It was a full five minutes before he came back.

"We can see the Chairman at his home," he said. "None of the other members of the Committee are available."

It wasn't exactly what Muldowney wanted. Instinctively he felt that for his own safety he needed to see all five members across the table once more. A report to a single member accompanied only by his devious superior offered a limited form of security but it was better than nothing.

He picked up Queally outside the GPO and drove out to the Security Committee head's address. As they were going past the Olympia theatre he told the spymaster about his experience with the stage hypnotist's leprechaun episode. Queally was amused. Muldowney felt that the whole thing was sick and that people had been made to look foolish, but the thing appealed to the perversity of Queally's nature.

241

The Chairman's home was a surprisingly modest semi detached house in an ordinary suburb. He received them in his shirt sleeves and brought them into the front room. A teenage daughter brought in tea and left the three men alone. The Chairman seemed far less formidable in these surroundings, but Muldowney was not deceived into thinking that he was any less implacable than he had been at the morning meeting. This was a stern hard man. Advancing years had brought no mellowing properties to his disposition.

Muldowney described the plot as he had been given it by Joyce Dolan. He named all the participants and outlined their roles. Queally stared at him in silent astonishment as he unfolded his narrative. It was a story which far outshone any of the myriad of trivial happenings with which the spymaster over the years had justified his existence.

The Chairman heard him out in silence. Once or twice he briefly interrupted to clarify a point. When Muldowney had finally finished there was silence for a moment. Queally stared transfixed at the Chairman. He half expected to be abused for failing to have presented this extraordinary affair from taking place in the first place, but the Chairman, if indeed he had at any stage been inclined to apportion blame, was no too deeply immersed in the intricacies of the situation.

"Is it your assessment that the gold is irrecoverable," he asked Muldowney.

The agent gave an affirmative nod.

"Can we be sure that the paintings will be delivered as promised."

Muldowney was less definite on this point. Certainly Joyce Dolan was absolutely sure and he communicated this to the Chairman with the warning that of course they were in the hands of unscrupulous men.

The Chairman considered the matter in silence for a time.

"I am inclined to agree that the paintings will come through," he said. "The vendors are obviously a highly organized group. They had enough influence in international financial circles to put tremendous pressure on the Irish government. This is what forced us to move the gold in the first place. They were resourceful enough to steal it on the way to Zurich."

"How did you find out that there was an organized run on the Irish currency," Muldowney asked curiously.

The Chairman smiled bleakly.

"The English bank official, Edgar, picked it up," he said. "He reported to Threadneedle street and the Foreign Office passed the information on to me."

Muldowney understood. As Minister for External Affairs, the Chairman was the official link between Ireland and Britain. The Security Committee had hatched a plot of its own to try and catch the conspirators when they drew down the gold in Switzerland. What they didn't understand was that they were up against a formidable if subterranean military machine which had no intention of letting the bullion get as far as Zurich. The Committee was pushed to the edge of a precipice. It had to kill the messenger to survive. The English banker had as good as signed his own death warrant when he did his duty and reported what he knew to his London office.

The Chairman was silent for a few moments while he considered further.

"I think we're safe enough," he said finally. "They will have other items to sell," he went on. "They won't want to get a

243

reputation for bilking people, particularly in a transaction of this size. That course of action would totally destroy their credibility for the future."

"Can anything be done through the German Embassy,' Queally asked.

The Chairman shook his head.

"We can have this attaché recalled, of course, and we could institute a hue and cry in Germany, but I am inclined to agree with Muldowney here. It would be counter productive."

"What will the situation be once we get our hands on the paintings," Muldowney queried.

The Chairman studied him speculatively for a moment.

"We would then be free, of course, go after the bullion by bringing in the German authorities," he said. "I doubt if the government would want to go public on the mater. If people were arrested it would get into the newspapers, here and abroad."

His assessment coincided with the one Muldowney had made an hour or two earlier. The secret agent complimented himself once again on his own judgment, but he probed further.

"I was thinking more about the legitimate ownership of the paintings," he said. "The German officers don't own them. They are looted property."

"Quite so," the minister agreed. "But how are we to establish their legitimate ownership. We have no means of contacting the owners. Indeed it is quite possible that some if not all of them are dead. The war has been over for nine years and they have not come forward."

Muldowney was tempted to comment that the Germans had made sure that there would be very few claimants by sending them to the death camps but said nothing. The Chairman continued with his appraisal of the situation.

"I think the balance of convenience on the matter dictates that the pictures are treated as the rightful property of the Irish government unless people come forward with provable claims which I doubt will happen. Our task now is to ensure that the pictures actually get here."

He looked expectantly at Muldowney. The agent was on less certain ground now.

"The arrangements are that they are to be handed over to Joyce Dolan and placed in the National Gallery," he said. "I have no reason to suppose that this is not going to happen."

"How can you be sure of this,' Queally interrupted testily, anxious to get back some of his lost dominance

The Chairman waved a hand at him to be quiet.

Muldowney spoke again.

"I have some concerns," he said. "I think that probably the pictures will arrive with the exhibition as arranged and will go to the National Gallery. I would be worried, however, that there might be some attempt to interfere by ..."

He paused deliberately and then went on "Other parties."

The Chairman said nothing for a moment.

"And who might these other parties be" he inquired in similarly quiet tones.

Muldowney went for the absent Finucane's jugular. It was payback time.

There is one member of the government who has played a certain role in this matter already," he said. "Not only was he prepared to blackmail your committee with the currency pressure and barter the nation's gold reserves but he was going to skim off the top as well."

The Chairman knew exactly who he was talking about.

"You think Finucane might try to take some of the paintings," he enquired. "Why not all of them"

Muldowney shook his head.

"They would be too difficult to dispose of," he said.

His long talk with Joyce Dolan had given him at least a sketchy inkling of how the art world functioned.

"It is one thing to have these paintings placed without question in the National Gallery as a permanent part of the collection," he said. "It is quite another to try and sell them on the open market. It would be very difficult."

"Dealers would require some sort of provenance and questions would certainly be asked about an Irishman coming on the scene with such a large consignment of European pictures," he went on. "Apart from which it would be a very dangerous thing to do. The Germans would kill him if they thought they had been compromised in any way. And you might kill him as well," he remarked looking straight at the Committee head.

If the shot got home, the Chairman gave no sign.

"You think he will go after one or two."

"He might, perhaps not even to sell them," Muldowney said. "He might just want to have something for his own collection."

He moved closer on his quarry.

"I have a list of the paintings," he said in a flash of understanding.

Now he suddenly understood the nature of the list of foreign names and dates.

"I will give this to the Committee in return for certain assurances."

Queally listened attentively. He immediately understood that Muldowney was referring to one of the unidentified schedules that had been included with the shipment documents. He decided not to indicate that he too had a copy.

"The man is a small time crook," the Chairman said abruptly. "He will be caught out sooner or later. We cannot unfortunately take any legal action against him if he gets his hands on some of these pictures, but there are other ways of dealing with him in connection with this whole affair. He will not be allowed to continue in politics."

He addressed Queally, more or less for the first time.

"Your department must ensure that the delivery of these pictures goes ahead as planned," he said. "The Irish woman, Dolan, and the German are free to carry through the operation. We can assume that the pictures will be safe once they are in the confines of the Gallery and catalogued as part of its collection. It will be your job to ensure that nothing happens to them on the way there. Finucane is not to profit from the matter. We will deal with him in due course."

He stood up. They were dismissed. Muldowney had one other issue to raise, however. Veronica was still in jail.

"One of my operatives was arrested," he said. "The police took her in while she was watching the bank at an early stage of the affair. She should be released."

The Chairman was slightly surprised at the sharpness of his tone, but wrote on a sheet of paper on which he had been making some other notes.

Queally intervened.

"There will be some problems with this," he said. "The police are anxious to keep this woman in custody. They have their own reasons. She has already made a court appearance and it will be difficult to get her released. She wasn't one of our official people," he added as a jibe at Muldowney.

The politician lookd sharply at the spymaster. He obviously detected some undercurrent in Queally's tone.

"We cannot interfere in the judicial process," he said. "The courts are totally independent. Matters will have to take their course."

Muldowney tried to argue but the Chairman waved them out of the room.

Muldowney decided to let the matter go for the moment. He had achieved quite a lot from this meeting as it was. Queally would be kept from going after Joyce Dolan and her German partner. Finucane would be severely dealt with. The murdered English bank official, however, would not be avenged. Muldowney had still not come to terms with the fact that the Security Committee had ordered his own death and that he had been sitting in the same room as the man who had authorized

248

his execution.

At the same time things were working out to some extent. It did not seem likely that he would be able to expose the Grim Grey Men for either the loss of the bullion or the murder of the English banker. These men were all powerful. But there was a better side to the affair. The country would retain the pictures which it was receiving in return for its missing bullion.

Muldowney had, he believed, also made his own position a little stronger. As long as he could deliver what he had promised, he was certainly certain that his life would be safe.

Chapter Sixteen

Queally sat alone across the table from the Grim Grey Men. He had listened in silence as the Chairman briefed his four colleagues on the report which Muldowney had made the night before.

"Our situation is this, gentlemen," he was concluding. "We have lost the bullion but the state is getting back some value for its money in terms of the paintings. We, of course, will have to satisfy ourselves in due course that these paintings are in fact authentic and as valuable as claimed. We have also to deal with one of our ministerial colleagues who was a key figure in orchestrating this affair from the Irish side, and who also tried to personally line his pockets."

He was silent for a moment. The naked contempt in his tones lingered on the air. He turned to Queally.

"The disciplining of our colleague will be a matter for ourselves," he said. "We have to accept that the German goes free. He is after all a diplomat with immunity. We have to decide the future of the National Gallery archivist, that Dolan woman, and your agent Muldowney."

He was silent for a moment again and the continued.

"My personal view is that Muldowney is a very dangerous man. He has succeeded in uncovering a vast amount of information in a very short space of time, which of course is a tribute to your training, Mr Queally," he added in a sardonic note of bogus praise. "But this agent in our service, in the country's service," he corrected, "has been responsible for the deaths of two people. We have to decide whether such a man can remain at liberty."

He could have added that Muldowney knew too much about the Chairman and his Committee.

THE IRISH SECRET AGENT

He addressed his colleagues.

"We have a major difficulty with this man," he said. "He holds evidence that would expose this whole affair. He has made it quite clear that if anything happens to him it will be released. We don't know how and up to now, Mr Queally" he lingered for a moment after speaking the spymaster's name, "has not been able to find out where this evidence has been retained."

"The evidence consists of a complete set of copies of the bullion shipment documents," he went on. "These disclose that we authorized the arrangements as well as the setting up of the numbered account opened for us in Switzerland by the Bank of England. In addition he has a complete list of the paintings which are coming here. This means that they could be identified at some stage in the future, and we and the country could be linked with their misappropriation."

"We cannot now kill this man," he went on. "In fact I withdrew that instruction a few days ago, but he must be silenced in some way."

He spoke directly to Queally.

"That is your decision," he said. "You must keep him alive but you have to neutralize him somehow, perhaps with promotion, perhaps, with money or indeed an illness requiring hospitalization."

He looked meaningfully across the table at the Section head.

Queally accepted his instructions without any comment. He had other matters, however, which had to be brought up.

"There are other loose ends," he said. "This woman, Veronica, is a protégé of Muldowney. He is determined that she should get out of jail."

The Chairman was no more now prepared to hear about Veronica than he had been the previous evening.

"She is nobody," he said. "She'll get parole in due course if she behaves herself in prison. In the meantime from our standpoint she's better off locked up. She can't talk to anyone about what she knows. The experience will give her a warning about what will happen if she gets out of line afterwards."

"And Cronin," the spymaster asked.

"Cronin is a different issue, altogether," the Chairman said. "You need not concern yourself with him any further. He has been transferred to another department. He has some special skills which are needed elsewhere."

Queally grasped the situation immediately. Cronin was someone else's man. He went back to his office in a state of some perturbation. It was highly disturbing to learn that Cronin had been a mole in his department, serving two masters. The big man was also obviously a state assassin controlled ultimately by someone else. The spymaster remembered his previous focus on his large hands and shuddered involuntarily. They were undoubtedly the hands which had choked the life out of the English bank official.

The time might come when he would be ordered to dispose of Queally in similar fashion. And now the man had a personal grudge. It was Queally who had put him in line for killing when the executioners had tried to eliminate Muldowney with their rolling coils of death.

Muldowney's future was top of his agenda. He made a number of calls in search of specific information he had to be certain that the procedure upon which he was determined to embark would work. One telephone call led to another until eventually he had secured all the information and contacts that he

252

required. Finally he had a name. His orders from the Grim Grey Men required the engagement of a specialist, a leader in his field. No ordinary run of the mill practitioner of the professional skills he required would do. The man selected would have to provide a service which he might not be too willing to grant.

Queally had created his department by knowing how certain things were done. He had also made his own very special kind of contacts over the years. A call to a well placed official in the Aliens Office secured him the favour that he needed. Within minutes three officers of that department were on their way across the city to make an arrest which threatened deportation.

Qually put down the telephone. He thought for a long time and finally left his office and walked across the city center towards the great sprawl of ornate magnificence that was Leinster House, the parliament building. That the state had been able to contain its parliament within its portals, and in addition house its cultural edifices, the National Library, National Museum and on the Merrion side, its National Gallery, was a monument to the sumptuousness and power of the princely earls of Leinster in bygone days. London had its House of Commons and commemorated the rise of the ordinary man. Dublin which had cast off the Crown evoked the memory of the past by settling comfortably in the palace of the erstwhile moguls.

Joyce Dolan was at work in the National Gallery when he arrived. Unlike Muldowney on his visit Queally asked for directions and was sent to Joyce's office, a small room out of sight of the public galleries.

He introduced himself and uncharacteristically got straight to the heart of his problem. She listened in silence to his assurances that the help that she had to give him would ensure

253

her own personal safety and freedom from any kind of encounter with the law. She would also be allowed to remain at work in the gallery. Her life would continue as before and she would have the additional pleasure of being in contact with the paintings which she had helped to install as part of her contribution to Irish culture.

Joyce Dolan had gone through a great deal in the past twenty four hours. He naive and golden hued view of her involvement in this curious contribution which was being made to the Irish cultural treasure chest had been rudely savaged by Muldowney's disclosure of the murder of the English bank official. Then had come the revelation that the project was known to other secret agents and to some senior members of the government. Her relationships with both Mannheim and Finucane were exposed and her cherished position in the National Gallery was under threat.

Queally's visit was disturbing but also brought her the promise of some relief. She was upset and concerned at what he had to propose, but Queally knew how to persuade, to cajole, to obliquely threaten, and to get his way. He excelled in circumstances where he had a vulnerable victim to pressurize. What she had to do would save Muldowney's life, he argued. The aspirations that she cherished so much would be secured if Muldowney could be brought into a situation where he no longer posed a threat to the state.

Queally, of course, had his own personal agenda. He desperately needed to put Muldowney down. This was the man he had brought from nowhere, whom he had petted and at the same time despised as his personal running dog. Muldowney had defied Queally's well honed system which drove agents to function on command and produce results that were tailored to the needs and policies of the service which Queally had endowed with its own mysterious purpose.

Muldowney had got out of the straight jacket of Queally's peculiar service. He had brought himself to the notice of the most important and powerful men in the state. He had influenced events, and above all had functioned so effectively that he had been able to wrong foot the spymaster and push him into a secondary role. Muldowney in fact had committed the most heinous sin of all, he had made his master appear incompetent.

The spymaster was under no illusion. The Grim Grey Men had noted every aspect, every nuance, of Muldowney's presentation. His underling had forced his way into the circle of power, and Queally had been diminished by his presence. Muldowney had to be destroyed, not just to safeguard the Security committee, but to ensure that Queally's career did not also come under threat.

Queally was a vicious, vengeful man. He did not accept such conduct lightly and in normal circumstances Muldowney would have been dismissed from the Section. But circumstances were far from normal. Queally himself had been subjected to one of the most traumatic episodes in his career when he had been exposed to the revelation that men could be killed by the state outside the judicial process. It was the first time that he had to deal with such an instruction. The spymaster excelled in deviousness but he was not by nature a violent man. Indeed cowardice ranked equally with deviousness in his makeup. But what he was proposing would have to rank as one of the most devious and complex ventures of is long period of service.

Joyce Dolan did her part. She rang Queally from her home later in the afternoon. Muldowney was with her now. The spymaster went to the outer office. A tall thin sun tanned man sat there flanked by the immigration officers. He was well dressed, in a tailored suit, expensive shirt, silk tie and costly cufflinks and tiepin. This was no ordinary down at heel asylum seeker who had come for a humdrum lifestyle on a few pounds of social welfare payment.

Queally spoke to him quietly but with sufficient menace in his tones to ensure that the man would fear for his future. The angry pent up protests which he had launched when Queally first approached died away as he listened to the spymaster. He was flattered by this special demand for his services.

"It can be done, of course," he said. "You were well advised to come to me. This is a matter which requires a very selective, very professional approach."

Queally nodded.

"I am told that you are the best in your field," he said. "This is your opportunity to prove it. You make a good living here," he went on quickly scanning the prisoner's opulent attire again. "If you oblige our government in this way you can remain."

Queally dismissed the immigration officers and led his companion down to his car. They arrived at Joyce Dolan's house within half an hour.

She let them in without a word. Her manner was vaguely hostile yet at the same time resigned.

Muldowney sat at ease in the front room. Queally introduced his companion vaguely as Viktor, and made some attempt at conversation. Muldowney listened idly to Queally. The spymaster talked but didn't really seem to have much to say that was of any interest.

The secret agent's eyes settled on the foreign looking visitor. He was an unusual companion for Queally and he wondered why the spymaster had brought him to Joyce Dolan's house.

He thought perhaps he might be an art expert brought in from overseas, and lazily decided to wait until Queally got around to tell him why he was there.

Muldowney's eyes strayed to the visitor again. He was swinging a small gold chain with some sort of pendant on the end of it. The chain dangled casually from one hand. It seemed to be just an idle habit. Muldowney's eyes followed the pendant for a moment or two and he heard the man begin to speak in a low but commanding voice. The tones became deeper and more intense. Muldowney struggled to make out the words, but he couldn't understand them. Then he heard nothing more.

The hypnotist put away his chain and pendant and spoke quietly to the spymaster.

"You can move him now," he said.

He glanced briefly at the unconscious Muldowney.

"When he wakes up he will have forgotten everything, even his career with your department. He will only remember his earlier life and the fact that he was a civil servant. He will never know that he was once a secret agent."